His Heart

Unforgettable 2

Niomie Roland

Contents

Lexi

"You're leaving?" I put down my amaretto sour and stared at Evie, my cousin by marriage, across the table. Next to Evie sat Rilya, also related to me by marriage.

My older sister, Tiffany, was married to Rilya and Evie's cousin, Allan. Though not related by blood, Evie, Rilya and I had become as close as sisters over the years.

Now, as Evie abruptly announced her departure, Rilya chimed in protest. "We made a pact!" I knew Rilya was disappointed, having looked forward to the rare kid-free night out with the girls.

It was Valentine's night, and our small group was enjoying a fine dinner at one of Montrose's upscale restaurants. For the last ten minutes, Evie had been more interested in texting rather than the conversation around the table, and then suddenly, she was looking for her purse and announcing her intention to leave.

My cousins and I had all found ourselves alone on love day and agreed to spend it together. After dinner, we planned on getting our groove on at the newly opened live music club nearby. We'd even booked hotel rooms nearby for the night.

"We promised to spend the evening together, have a little girl time," added Kneshel, who was seated next to me.

Kneshel was married to Rilya's older brother, Monty. Unlike Rilya and me, Kneshel seemed less miffed about Evie's decision to bail. I suspected Kneshel was hopeful of Lamont showing up to Montrose, despite being on a work trip.

"I know!" Evie agreed. She had enough grace to look contrite, but waved her cell phone around as if it was evidence. "Darius apologized for breaking up with me last night. He felt bad he couldn't afford to buy me a gift. But he said he realizes now he is the only gift I need."

Rilya and I exchanged a look and next to me, Kneshel snorted. Just this morning, Evie wailed over brunch about what a thoughtless jerk Darius was. Now, a few texts had her sprinting back into his fickle arms?

"He's not normally like this!" Evie defended her man. "Deep down he's a teddy bear." She pouted.

I could see Evie's mistake from a mile away. Darius wasn't worth her time, but I knew better than to voice my concerns. She'd figure it out eventually. At least, I hoped she would.

"If that's what you want, then go ahead," I said, my tone even as I brushed my hair back, more out of habit than necessity

Hurriedly, Evie trotted around the table, giving apologetic hugs and air-kisses. "I hope my favorite cousin's wife..." she glanced at Kneshel.

"Favorite cousin?" Rilya repeated in amazement, shaking her head.

"...Will be kind enough to cover my tab," Evie said chirpily. "Cause I'm just a penniless student and she's a doctor." Then we watched as she scurried out on high heels. "I'll make it up to you!" she yelled over her shoulder as she went.

"What am I? Chopped liver?" Rilya said long after Evie disappeared.

Kneshel laughed and jokingly patted her hand. "You know she loves you."

Rilya snorted.

I wasn't surprised. "She's true to her name," I said. "Effervescence."

Evie was the youngest of the Lewis cousins, the most spoiled and the most free-spirited. Her inexperience with romantic love showed.

"Nothing keeps her down for long," Kneshel agreed. "Let's hope your parents aren't dealing with as much drama babysitting our children tonight."

Rilya groaned. "Oh lord, don't remind me. Leaving my baby girl for a night is hard enough. I hope Mom and Dad still have their sanity intact when we get back."

The women chuckled. Rilya's parents had offered to babysit their granddaughters as a Valentine's treat.

Kneshel turned to face me. "Baby talk aside. How are things with you and Ben? You don't speak about him much."

Rilya leaned in, concern in her eyes. "And you're in Montrose with us versus staying back in Valleyfield to wait till he gets off shift. What's really going on between you two?"

"We're fine," I said, too quickly.

I could tell by the look in Kneshel's eyes she wasn't entirely convinced, but I didn't offer more. My relationship with Ben wasn't something I wanted to unpack here, not in this setting. It was... complicated, and tonight wasn't about complications.

Seemingly convinced by my assurances about Ben, Kneshel said, "Well, I'm glad you're here with us tonight."

As I sipped my drink, I relaxed, grateful the conversation had moved on from my love life. Kneshel and Rilya were my best friends, but there were some things I preferred to keep to myself. My relationship with Ben was one of them.

Tonight was for enjoying time with my cousins, not rehashing my romantic life. Rilya launched into a funny story about her students, and soon the women were giggling together.

As I mulled over my cousin's earlier questions about Ben, the arrival of a tall man with a rich brown complexion in the restaurant tossed any thought of Ben out of my head. The man's frame filled the doorway. Faint light glinted off his black-rimmed glasses as his gaze swept the room. His head was shaved close, his beard neatly trimmed.

I glanced up and caught his gaze for a moment longer than I intended. A faint heat simmered beneath my skin, but I looked away, unwilling to give too much away.

From the corner of my eye, I saw a hostess glide toward the stranger with practiced charm. His gaze shifted away from me as he exchanged a few words with the hostess.

From the man's expression, it was clear he didn't have a reservation. Which meant he would likely be turned away from the packed restaurant.

As he turned to leave, I scanned his strong features, trying to imprint them in my memory. I knew it was silly to feel disappointed. He was a stranger, and I would never see him again.

I forced myself to tune back into the conversation at my table. But my mind kept wandering, replaying those intense moments of eye contact over and over.

Suddenly, Kneshel jolted from her seat, waving her hand excitedly. "MJ! Over here!" she called out.

I turned to see Kneshel rushing over to greet the handsome stranger. Kneshel gave him an enthusiastic hug before linking her arm in his and leading him to our table.

"That's Marcus Davis... Junior," Rilya explained. "Hazel and Trina's brother."

There was no time for further discussion as Kneshel and Marcus approached our table. "Look who I found!" she announced breathlessly.

I was looking.

This man was finer up close, with a strong jawline and broad shoulders tapered to a trim waist. His muscular build was evident even under his tailored suit.

Marcus turned his attention to me, his eyes locking with mine. "I don't believe we've met before. I'm MJ and you are?"

I paused for a moment, my mind suddenly blank. "I'm... I'm Lexi," I stammered out, feeling a blush creep up on my cheeks.

He extended his hand across the table towards me. As our hands connected, a sudden jolt coursed through my body, igniting every nerve ending.

"Nice to meet you, Lexi." He held my gaze for a beat too long before letting go.

"Likewise," I managed to reply, my heart fluttering in my chest. Oh no, I definitely could not afford another complication in my life, and the air around this one screamed trouble.

He turned his attention to Rilya, shook her hand and then sat in Evie's vacated seat. "Thank you for inviting me to join your table. I didn't remember it was Valentine's Day."

I was surprised to hear an attractive man like Marcus was alone on Valentine's Day. I wondered if he was single, then chided myself for my thoughts. The waiter arrived and took a dinner order from Marcus and dessert order from us.

"Are you headed to Valleyfield?" Kneshel asked MJ after the waiter swept away our orders.

"No," he replied, leaning back in his chair. He explained he'd arrived in Montrose earlier in the day for a meeting and would fly back to Singapore the next day.

My eyes widened in surprise. *Singapore?* I studied Marcus with fresh curiosity, wondering what kind of work had taken him to such a distant land. I ached to know more about him, but held my tongue, not wanting to pry.

"Jet-setter like your sister," Kneshel said with an impressed whistle.

An easy grin spread across Marcus' face, causing desire to course through me. I inhaled the subtle citrus notes of his cologne as he reached for one of the dinner rolls in the center of the table.

"Must be fascinating experiencing a whole different culture," Rilya remarked.

"It's been an eye-opening journey," he replied.

Then he launched into vivid descriptions of Singapore's chaotic night markets alive with enticing aromas, the city's gleaming financial district, and fusion cuisine. The subtle baritone of his voice made my skin prickle.

I leaned in, chin propped on my hand, absorbed in his account. The candlelight cast a warm glow on his smooth brown skin and caught the flecks of amber in his dark eyes. I could almost taste the mouthwatering dishes he described.

"It sounds incredible," I breathed, our gazes locking. "I wouldn't mind experiencing the markets and sampling all the amazing street food one day."

"Singapore is a fascinating city," Marcus said, leaning in closer. "But it's not the sights that make it special. It's the way it makes you feel alive, energized, and ready to take on the world. I'd love to show you what I mean someday."

For a moment, the clatter of dishes and the hum of conversation around us faded away. The thought of exploring a dazzling foreign city with him made my heart beat faster with both anticipation and nerves.

A moment later, the waiter appeared, balancing a tray of desserts and Marcus' braised short ribs. I let out a silent breath of relief for the distraction.

I busied myself scooping some of the crème brûlée onto my spoon, avoiding Marcus' stare across the table. Rilya and Kneshel chatted casually about how good their dessert tasted while I tried to rein in my erotic thoughts.

The sound of raucous laughter from a nearby table jolted my head up, and I spotted Monty weaving his way between the tables, his face split by a grin and a bouquet clutched in one hand. Kneshel was all but dancing with excitement before they were in each other's arms and making out.

I had harbored a crush on Monty when we were younger, but he never thought of me as more than a cousin. When he started dating Trina, I knew it was time to move on. After things with Trina crumbled, Monty found love with Kneshel. Witnessing their genuine connection, I let go of my lingering feelings.

"Eww, bro!" Rilya protested, interrupting their reunion. "No need to scar me!"

Lamont pulled back, unfazed. "Then you'll be glad to know I'm here to steal your sister-in-law away." He gave her a roguish wink. His hungry gaze drank Kneshel in as he greeted Marcus, who was tucking away his food.

Kneshel gathered her things, grin wide at her husband's amorous surprise. I sighed inwardly, lamenting the dwindling party but unable to begrudge their romantic night.

"I know I'm stealing your fun third wheel away," Lamont said ruefully, eliciting a playful swat from his wife. "Let me make it up to you, ladies." He withdrew a sleek platinum card from his wallet and placed it on the table. "Tonight's on me. It's the least I can do for crashing your party."

Rilya's eyes lit up when she picked up the card, turning it over in her hands. "I hope your credit limit can handle the damage we'll do."

Laughing and clinging to each other, Lamont and Kneshel made their way between the tables toward the door. I watched as Lamont swept his wife into another passionate kiss before exiting the restaurant.

I leaned back with a wistful smile, happy for my friend, but envious of the obvious love between the two. I wondered if a love like theirs would ever come my way. My musings were interrupted by Rilya.

"I can't believe our fearsome foursome has dwindled down to just us, because our cousin and my sister-in-law chose to spend the night with ball carriers instead of us," said Rilya.

Marcus' eyebrows shot up in amusement. He chuckled, raising his hands in mock surrender.

"No offense to present company," Rilya added.

"We should—" I started, but the sound of Rilya's phone interrupted my suggestion for us to call it a night.

Marcus' gaze found mine across the table. I felt the heat creep up my neck as his eyes lingered on my lips for a second too long before flicking back up to meet mine. My breath hitched, and an unspoken tension crackled between us.

I crossed my legs under the table, the movement drawing his attention before he returned to his food with a knowing smirk, as if he was enjoying the effect he had on me.

I was still trying to steady the flutter of my pulse when Rilya's voice cut through the moment, pulling me back to reality. "It was my dad. Sunny has a fever."

Rilya's daughter, Sunny, was five months old, and I was the only person in the family who knew the identity of Sunshine's father. I had unexpectedly walked in on them kissing during Kneshel and Lamont's wedding reception. I had been sworn to secrecy by Rilya.

"I need to be with her," Rilya added, gathering her purse and coat.

"Of course," I said. As Rilya gathered her things, I glanced around for the server. "Let me handle the check," I added.

"Don't cut your night short because I have to go. Stay, enjoy your night off!"

I felt my cheeks warm. "Oh, I shouldn't…"

"I'd be honored if you'd stay and keep me company," Marcus interjected. "Seems a shame to dine alone on Lover's Day."

"I… well, I suppose I could stay a little longer. It would be a shame to waste Lamont's generous offer." I paused, my eyes meeting Marcus' before darting away. "And you're right, no one should have to dine alone on Valentine's Day."

After wishing us a good evening, Rilya rushed away. I sank back into my seat, suddenly aware of the intimate atmosphere enveloping Marcus and me. The restaurant seemed to dim, leaving only the soft glow of candlelight illuminating our table.

I snuck a glance at him, taking in his strong profile. Warmth—exhilarating and nerve-wracking—spread through my veins when I noticed him watching me. Unsure what to say, I traced the rim of my glass as silence descended the table.

Marcus moved his dinner plate aside and leaned forward, his forearms resting on the tablecloth. "Tell me more about yourself, Lexi."

It was the first time I'd heard him say my name. I liked the way it sounded on his lips.

"What do you want to know?" I asked, willing my voice not to tremble.

"Everything," was his response.

I became aware of our knees touching under the tablecloth. I rubbed my sweaty palms on the napkin in my lap, hoping he couldn't sense my nervousness. This man's nearness was doing strange things to my composure.

"I'm not interesting."

Marcus leaned in. "I find it hard to believe," he murmured.

I fidgeted with my napkin, then met his gaze. "Oh?"

"You seem like someone with a wealth of experiences. I'd love to hear about your life."

His genuine interest caught me off guard, and I opened up. "Well, there's not much to tell, really, but..." I paused, gathering my thoughts. "I suppose I could give you the Lexi Voss highlight reel."

I told him of my lifelong roots in Valleyfield and my nursing career. Marcus listened, nodding along as I spoke about spending most of my free time with my family.

I didn't mention my relationship with Ben. It was private, too personal to dump on someone I barely knew. "The furthest I've traveled from Valleyfield is to Montrose." I shrugged. "It's a pretty simple life."

"Simple can be beautiful," he said. "It takes courage to find contentment where you are instead of constantly seeking more."

His perspective on my life in Valleyfield was refreshing. Living in the same small town year after year, it was easy for me to feel like I was missing out on adventures happening elsewhere.

When I saw posts of friends traveling abroad or moving to big cities, pangs of envy sometimes pierced my contentment. I couldn't help but to wonder if there was more out there for me beyond familiar streets and lifelong neighbors.

I tilted my head. "What about you? What drew you to Singapore?"

"After Harvard Law, I didn't want to take the safe route. I needed something bigger, something challenging. Singapore was the place where I could push myself. The city's energy hooked me right away, and I've been chasing it ever since."

There was something magnetic about the way he spoke, as if every word was part of a larger plan I couldn't quite see yet. I could tell Marcus wasn't the type to settle for a job or, I suspected, for anything else.

"What's this club Rilya and Kneshel were discussing earlier?" he asked.

"It's a live music club. We'd hoped to go there after dinner," I said, hoping he didn't hear the disappointment in my tone.

"Let's go to the club. You want to check it out, right?"

His tone wasn't demanding, but there was a certain finality in the way he spoke, like he had already decided for both of us.

"I'd love to," I said, surprised at how excited I felt.

I wasn't in the habit of following strangers to clubs, but something about Marcus made me feel... curious. Besides, it was Valentine's Day, and I had promised myself I'd have some fun.

With our decision made, Marcus settled our entire dinner bill, and we made our way out into the chilly night air.

MJ

I placed my hand at the small of Lexi's back, enjoying the feel of her warm skin under my fingers. Her small waist contrasted with dramatically flared hips, forming a silhouette surpassing even an hourglass. She was a full foot shorter than I was, which stirred my deepest desires and led to all many raunchy imaginings.

A quiet chuckle escaped me, the sound lost in the noisy downtown streets. It suddenly struck me she was here with me.

When I had asked her to join me at the club, I knew she would agree. There was a spark between us from the moment we locked eyes, and I wouldn't let her slip away.

As we walked, I marveled at how drastically my evening had changed course. Earlier, when Kneshel had spotted me at the restaurant, I'd been mildly annoyed. I'd hoped to get in and out of Montrose incognito, unprepared to deal with any familiar faces on this trip.

My family didn't know I was in the U.S., and I didn't want to share my reasons for being here in case things didn't pan out. But my mood had significantly improved when I realized Kneshel was sharing the table with the woman who'd intrigued me almost as soon as I walked into the restaurant.

Lexi was different.

I'd sensed it the moment we'd first made eye contact and confirmed it the second I touched her. Her features enchanted me: round cheeks, a pointed chin, and skin of a flawless, even brown tone.

While the conversation at our table had included all three women, it was Lexi who intrigued me. The quiet confidence in her smile, the way she seemed to observe more than speak.

I could tell there was more beneath the surface, and I wanted to understand it. She wasn't attention-seeking like the women I usually encountered. No, Lexi was different.

I'd hung on to her every word, fascinated by the glimpses of her personality. I could tell she was shy, but I found it endearing and looked forward to drawing her out of her shell.

My gaze had lingered on her, tracing the contours of her face, the delicate way she held her glass. I memorized the cadence of her laugh, the gentle way she looked away when she caught me staring, as if I could somehow preserve these fleeting moments like photographs in my mind.

It made me want to extend our evening and get to know Lexi on a deeper level. As we walked to the club from the restaurant, I intentionally kept the conversation light, hoping to put her at ease.

I made a game of pointing out silly things. The way a store sign was crooked, or the cat perched precariously on a windowsill looking utterly perturbed by our existence.

As we turned onto the street where the club was located, I noticed my hotel across the way. The proximity was convenient, but I pushed the thought aside, focusing instead on Lexi.

I wanted her to be comfortable and hear her laugh. The sound was becoming addictive.

The club was housed in a converted brick warehouse, keeping many of the original architectural elements, like exposed steel beams and ornate trusses high above. Wisps of hazy smoke lingered near the ceiling, drifting lazily through flashing lights illuminating a sea of dancing bodies underneath.

As I led Lexi into the club, the pulsating beat washed over us. The air was thick and heady, carrying the mingled scents of champagne, sweat, and perfume.

"Up front or in the back?" I leaned in close so she could hear me over the bassline.

"Back," she answered, then added, "but high up so we can see the stage."

I weaved us expertly through the crowd, tracing a path towards the mezzanine level where dim booths ringed a lowered dance floor. Below, fluorescent dance poles cast rippling shadows across ecstatic faces.

We rounded the final turn to find our booth, tucked discreetly in an alcove above the noise and chaos. Soft leather seats wrapped around a polished concrete table. I helped Lexi into her seat and sat beside her.

"What do you think? Good spot to take it all in?"

Lexi grinned, eyes bright even in the dim lighting. The diamond nose ring on her left nostril and the stud on her right eyebrow glinted. "It's perfect. I feel like I'm in the VIP lounge!" She laughed, settling back against the plush cushions as colorful lights danced across her features.

"What were you saying about a Valentine's Day pact?"

Before she could answer, a server appeared to take our orders. I ordered an aged Scotch and couldn't help but notice she ordered a virgin cosmopolitan. I listened as she explained how her three cousins by marriage had found themselves alone on this lover's night and agreed to spend it together.

"You don't have a boyfriend or a husband somewhere?"

Lexi told me she was single, and I found it surprising. She was a beautiful woman and smart, too. "What about you?" she asked.

"No boyfriend or husband," I answered dryly.

Lexi's mouth formed a perfect O, and I winked at her. She swatted my arm, laughing along with me.

"I'm single," I assured her once our laughter died down. "I don't do relationships." I hoped my response didn't sound bitter. I saw the flare of curiosity in her eyes and added, "My work keeps me busy."

Lexi didn't delve deeper, and I was grateful. I didn't want to explain my mistrust of the fairer sex...apart from my sisters, of course. Them, I held in high esteem even though they were borne from and raised by a woman who had little respect for propriety.

My mind drifted back to the night of my high school graduation when I saw my mother making out with Thomas Wesson, the local grocer, and my mother's married boss. I told dad about it and the man assured me he would handle it.

He never did. I had moved away for school, vowing never to set foot back in the town or speak to my mother.

The announcer's voice cut over the music and my dark musings. I was grateful for the interruption. Reminiscing about my family's past was never fun. Lexi and I turned toward the stage as a local hip-hop group stepped up to enthusiastic welcoming applause.

"I love hip-hop," she mouthed across to me as the band struck up.

"So do I," I responded, wondering if Lexi could be more perfect.

The playlist was a treasure trove of early 2000s hits, and soon the audience joined in, with Lexi and me among them. When the lead singer began spitting lyrics to a thudding drum line, Lexi shot to her feet and began gyrating her hips to the rhythm, and the artists became the second most interesting thing in the room. I couldn't drag my roving eyes from her undulating body or stop the tightening of my trousers.

I barely noticed the server arriving, balancing a tray with our drinks. Before the woman could set them down, an inebriated man stumbled into her.

My hand shot out, steadying the waitress before she could hit the table. By some miracle, none of the drinks spilled. I smiled at her as she set the drinks down and thanked me, but my attention was already shifting back to Lexi.

"Impressive reflexes? Because your reflexes are superhero level."

I smiled back at her. "We superheroes never tell. It's part of our prime directive."

"Prime directives are for robots," she pointed out sternly.

"I stand corrected."

The hip-hop group ended their set to cheers and were replaced by a jazz country band mellow enough for us both to take our seats and speak at an almost conversational level. As much as I'd enjoyed watching her dance, I was eager to talk to her.

I studied the expressive animation of Lexi's features as she spoke about her job as a nurse, chatting animatedly about the patients she cared for. I listened with fascination, charmed by the passion in her voice when she described her niece and nephew's antics.

I could tell nurturing and caring came naturally to her. Lexi's effusive personality and infectious laughter captivated me. I found myself wanting to share more of my own experiences with her, despite the inherent risk of becoming attached.

"I've got two fur babies." She glowed as she said it, and I half expected her to whip out her phone and start showing me photos. I was ready to bet they had their own Instagram profile.

"Their names are Kung and Fu," she supplied.

I was taken by surprise and tried not to grin. "Interesting names."

"There was a spike in burglaries a while back and I signed up for a martial arts class. Unfortunately, I never got the hang of it." She made a face. "I'm not the most coordinated person."

"You're lying," I challenged, thinking of the way she'd been rotating her hips not ten minutes before.

She let the compliment go and said, "So I got myself two deadly protectors."

"Smart. What breed are they? Bullies? German Shepherds? Dobermans?"

She coughed before responding, "Yorkshire terriers."

I stared at her for a bit, wondering if she was serious. Her eyes averted, and she bit her bottom lip to suppress a smile. I couldn't stop my burst of laughter, and she joined in. "I'm sure they'll shred any ankles you."

When our mirth subsided, she eyed me, then looked away with a serious expression. "What's wrong?"

"Maybe I shouldn't broadcast to strange men about my lack of self-defense skills."

"You're safe with me. I'll make sure of it."

Lexi's shoulders relaxed as she nodded, seeming to trust my sincerity. "Do you have any pets?" she asked. "Or kids?"

I chuckled, shaking my head. "No kids for me," I said, and I could have sworn she looked relieved by the news. "As for pets, I've never had one, not even growing up. Though I once wanted a parrot."

Lexi giggled, the sound melodic to my ears. "A parrot?"

I grinned sheepishly. "I thought it would be fun to have a talking bird. But my mom said birds were too messy and loud."

"Aww, too bad," Lexi said, her full lips turning down in a pretty pout, making me imagine all the things I could do with her mouth. The air hummed as I moved closer, drawn in by the gravitational pull of her presence.

My thoughts were a whirlpool with Lexi at the center, the rest of the world blurring at the edges. Falling for her would be unwise, but I felt helpless against the desire to make her mine.

Changing gears in my mind, I told her about my love of hiking mountain trails while she confessed her obsession with fancy cocktails. She talked about wanting to see the Northern Lights someday and I mentioned going scuba diving the previous summer.

"Sounds amazing." Her tone was wistful. "I've always wanted to scuba dive, but I've never even seen the ocean."

"Really?" I asked in surprise. When she shook her head, I leaned forward eagerly. "You would love it. Diving in the coral reefs is like entering a different world. The fish and coral are stunning."

Lexi's eyes were shining as I described the dazzling underwater sights. "The closest I've come to snorkeling is visiting the aquarium right here in Montrose. I got to see all the fish without getting wet."

I couldn't help but imagine the possibilities of her body wet and warm—her drenched hair sticking to her skin, her eyes shining like precious jewels in the depths of the ocean. My mind raced from the mundane to the erotic, from the plausible to the fantastical.

"Let's dance!"

"Me?" I shook my head. "The way I stomp around, you'd be looking for a personal injury lawyer afterward."

Lexi's eyes glinted mischievously. "I'll take my chances," she insisted. Her delicate fingers encircled my wrist, soft against my skin. She gave a playful tug, the honeyed scent of her perfume wafting over me as she led me away from the table.

"I'm warning you," I protested, pushing my glasses farther up my nose. "The last time I tried to dance, my friends had me tested for mad cow disease."

"I'm up for the challenge," she announced, and the lesson began.

As we began moving together, each brush of her hand against me sent a current racing through my veins, my skin tingling with the awareness of her proximity. Up close, I noticed the perfection of her teeth. Strands of her dark, glossy hair clung to the sheen of sweat on her graceful neck. I was tempted to lick it.

Try as I might, my movements remained awkward and clumsy compared to Lexi's natural rhythm. Her hands slid to my hips, brows arching in gentle teasing as she guided me.

"Well, I rarely use the word hopeless," she began. "But occasionally, exceptions must be made."

"I warned you." I chuckled and pulled her voluptuous frame against me.

Her body molded seamlessly to mine, curves cushioned against muscle. I delighted at her deep inhale and the movement of her hands on my shoulders.

"At least you didn't step on my toes."

"The night is still young. I make no promises."

"I suppose I'll have to keep my toes tucked in then," she quipped. The teasing lilt in her voice made my body stiffen.

"If you hold me closer, I'm less likely to go staggering around," I suggested.

"That right?" she asked archly, but her face was tilted toward mine and she looked amused.

Those lips.

Her smile.

Sometimes the angels themselves put opportunities in your path, and you had to seize them.

I was ensnared by this spirited woman in my arms. By the way she bit her lower lip to suppress a smile, eyes shining up at me. I brushed my thumb across her cheekbone.

Lexi leaned into my touch, lashes fluttering. I felt the quickening of her breath, the tremor going through her as I trailed my fingers along the curve of her jaw.

"Lexi..." Her name escaped me in a ragged whisper.

My pull toward her defied logic, but I didn't care. This was about more than desire. It was about discovering something worth pursuing. I wanted her, and I was determined to feel those soft lips against my own.

I ran my thumb over her bottom lip. She inhaled deeply, lips parting further in invitation. I hesitated only a moment before dipping my head. It felt like a journey of a thousand steps. Our noses grazed, breaths mingling.

Just before our lips met, Lexi pulled back. Confusion flickered in her eyes. "I..."

As much as I loved her voice, I silenced her protest with my index finger.

Lexi trembled against me but didn't pull away. Heart hammering, I closed the whisper of distance between us and her lips were against mine. It was a jolting, stunning sensation of contact.

The club, the music, everything fell away until there was only the taste of her. Firecrackers went off in my head, loud strings of popping noises.

This couldn't be real, I thought. It was one kiss. No way such a gentle contact could cause havoc on my entire being.

But it did.

I suddenly felt everything, sensed everything. The movement of her supple body against mine, the way she undulated to the music, which currently penetrated my core. I was no longer just hearing it. It was part of me.

This woman I hadn't known existed four hours before flowed through me. I had a momentary desire to pull away and break this connection because it confounded me.

But my hunger for her was intense, physical, and I knew she felt my arousal pressing against her stomach. I felt a soft puff of air against my face as she broke the kiss to sigh, the sound carrying a sense of surrender.

Placing my hands on her hips, I pulled her closer still. Her arms rose languorously to my shoulders. I felt every curve of hers against me. The arch of her back, the swell of her breasts against my chest, the heat of her body seeping through the thin fabric of her dress.

Her lips were soft, pliant under mine. The taste of her was everything I'd imagined and more. The sweet scent of her perfume mixed with the natural fragrance of her skin had me intoxicated.

Our tongues danced together, exploring each other. The kiss went on, a rhythm matching the throbbing beat of my heart.

The fire inside me was now an inferno, fueled by the taste of her lips, the feel of her body against mine, and the heady mix of arousal and desire pulsing through my veins. I'd kissed women before, but this was different.

This was devouring and consuming.

Lexi

When we finally pulled apart, my fingers instinctively brushed my lips. I felt branded by his touch, as if I no longer belonged entirely to myself. How could a single kiss make me feel like my whole world had shifted?

Sure, Marcus was handsome, well-dressed, articulate, and undeniably successful—a catch by any woman's standards. But the way he kissed me, the way he ignited a flame inside me I'd never felt before? It was completely unexpected.

I had always been a woman of reason, someone who relied on logic and rationale as my closest allies. But Marcus stirred something within me, creating an upheaval threatening everything I once believed about passion and romance.

We were still swaying to the music, but it felt like we were moving to our own private rhythm. His eyes were locked on mine, and I had the dizzying sense the kiss had affected him as deeply as it had me.

"Are you alright?" Marcus asked.

"I..." I began, but the words faltered, lost in the storm his kiss had sparked inside me. Instead, I nodded, probably too vigorously.

I ran my tongue across my lips, and his eyes followed the movement. My face heated, and I looked away, imagining exactly what thoughts my gesture had stirred in him.

Then he leaned in, his stubbled cheek brushing against mine as his mouth found the sensitive spot beneath my earlobe. He bit down, sending a jolt straight to my core. I whimpered, clutching at him. "Do you want to get out of here?"

I knew exactly what would happen if we left together. The tension had been building between us, but was this really what I wanted?

I'd always prided myself on being level-headed, cautious. This wild, impulsive desire wasn't me.

But the thought of walking away felt wrong. It wasn't only lust pulling me toward him; it was something deeper, something I couldn't quite explain...

I hesitated for a moment longer, reminding myself of the consequences. But maybe, this once, I could let go. One night wouldn't change who I was, right?

I looked into his eyes and nodded. I wanted him from a place deep inside me, even if it was only for a few hours.

"I'm a lawyer, Lexi. In this current climate, I need your words. I need to hear you say yes."

"There's a hotel right across the street," I managed, though my voice felt foreign to me. I hoped the hotel was nicer inside than its unremarkable exterior.

"That's where I'm staying," he replied.

"Well, how about that for a coincidence?" I said with a smile.

Marcus smiled back at me, a devilish glint in his eyes. "We'll call it serendipity," he said, reaching into his pocket, withdrawing a money clip from which he peeled several large bills and dropped them onto the table.

The gesture was casual, with no hint of showing off. It was the same graciousness he'd displayed when he'd paid for our dinner.

Then, with a boyish grin, he grabbed my hand. I clasped my fingers around his, enjoying the warmth of his palm, and the way my fingers disappeared into his. I allowed him to lead me through the crowd, which was growing denser as more people filed in to listen to the music, and out onto the sidewalk.

"It's raining!" I marveled, looking up.

The downfall wasn't heavy, but already the road was slick and glittering from reflected lights all around us. The sight pleased me immensely.

"Ready?" Marcus asked me, and then without waiting for an answer, broke into a jog, tugging me along with him into the road.

I could feel the splash of water on my ankles, and briefly worried about the damage it could do to my shoes. I spent an entire paycheck on them.

When we were halfway across the street, barely past the dividing lines painted in the road, I halted. Marcus turned to look me over.

"You okay?" he asked. "Did you change your mind? Because if you have, it's okay…"

I shook my head.

He looked relieved, then jokingly asked, "Want me to carry you?"

I lifted my face to the sky, feeling the droplets fall and roll down my cheek. "It's just…and this is going to sound stupid. But I've always wanted to be kissed in the rain—"

Marcus swooped down to claim my lips, right there in the middle of the road. I was lucky the current zinging between us wasn't electric, because given the water cascading all around us, I was sure I'd have received a shock strong enough to drop me.

I felt every fiber of my body respond with intense hunger. Even as the water trickled down my neck and soaked my clothes, I felt waves of heat roll over me.

His lips and tongue were expert, teasing, hungry, commanding. When he lifted me without effort, I wrapped my legs around his hips, glad for the chance to feel his hardness pressing between my legs where I wanted him most.

The blare of a car horn startled me and I slipped from his arms, but his hold on me prevented me from landing on my butt. The angry driver swerved around us, sending water splashing us. He rolled down his window and cursed us soundly.

Another driver with a car headed in the opposite direction yelled, "Get the fuck out the street and get a room!"

"I have a room!" Marcus yelled back, and I giggled.

"Let's go," I suggested, "before we get flattened."

Marcus nodded in agreement and got me safely to the other side and into the hotel. Once we were inside, he led me past reception, our damp clothes leaving a trail of droplets on the plush carpet.

"Fifth floor," he let me know.

The elevator doors closed, and Marcus's hand dropped lower, pulling me closer. I felt the heat of his touch through the damp fabric, but instead of leaning into the intensity, I took a breath, letting the moment linger.

I wasn't used to moving so fast, to feeling so much so quickly. But Marcus' hands were like flames as they moved across the slick fabric, leaving warmth in their wake across my goose-pimpled flesh.

He brushed a wet strand of hair off my forehead. I groaned internally at having to redo my newly installed weave.

Marcus looked down at me, his dark eyes twinkling under the dim lights of the lift. A droplet of rainwater slid down his cheek. His gaze centered on my lips, and I knew what he was thinking.

"You're addictive," he murmured before pressing his lips against mine. The kiss was gentle at first but soon engulfed like a wildfire.

I tasted the faint hint of rainwater on his skin. The clean taste mingled with the intoxicating flavor of his passion. My hands circled his neck, fingers brushing the wet hair at the base of his neck, as I lost myself in the sweet oblivion of our passion.

The elevator dinged, and the doors slid open. Marcus led me out without breaking our kiss, fumbling around a bit before producing a key card from his pocket.

With a beep and a soft click, the door opened, and we stumbled into the room, still locked in our embrace. The room was dimly lit by the outside street lights streaming in through the partly drawn blinds.

Marcus kicked the door shut behind him, his hands moving to unbutton my sodden coat. He pushed it off my shoulders and it fell to the carpeted floor with a soft thud. His drenched suit jacket followed my coat. His mouth moved over mine, exploring passionately while his hands found my waist, pulling me closer.

Without breaking our kiss, Marcus guided us toward the room on the right. I felt the edge of the bed against my knees, and then we were falling back onto the soft mattress, our rain-slicked bodies entwined. He removed his glasses with one hand and placed them on the side table.

His skillful hands moved over my body and a soft moan escaped me as his fingers found the hem of my damp dress, inching it upward. His touch was agonizingly slow, each movement igniting my skin as he explored me with an intimate familiarity.

"God, Lexi..." he groaned against my neck, his desire for me unmistakable as it pressed against my thigh. I fumbled with the buttons of his shirt, finally exposing the hard expanse of his chest. He shrugged the shirt off fully, and I traced the taut muscles beneath my fingers, feeling them flex under my touch.

His mouth found mine again in a breathless kiss. Every stroke of his tongue against mine sent waves of pleasure through me, and I matched his urgency, eagerly meeting his pace until we were both gasping for breath.

With skilled fingers, Marcus undid the zip at the back of my dress, pulling the fabric down to reveal my lingerie-clad body. His eyes darkened appreciatively as he took in my black, lace-covered form. His fingertips traced the delicate fabric, causing a delicious sensation to move through my body.

"Beautiful," he rasped, his voice heavy with desire, hands cupping my curves reverently. He lowered his head, leaving a trail of delicate kisses down my throat to my collarbone, sending rivulets of pleasure through my veins.

I gasped, arching into him when his mouth found the swell of my breast over the fabric. He teased me, teeth grazing lightly over the sensitive peak before giving it a soft nip.

His hands were on the move again, slipping beneath the lace to cup my bare skin. I sighed against his lips, wrapping my legs around him and pulling him closer.

"Patience," he murmured, his voice low and husky, promising nights of endless pleasure and mornings filled with whispered sweet nothings. But patience was the last thing on my mind. I wanted him right here, right now, raw and unfiltered.

I pulled away and sat up, my fingers teasing the front clasp of my bra. A coy smile played on my lips as I kept my eyes locked on his. With a soft click, the clasp popped open, and I let the lace fall to the bed.

Marcus groaned, his pupils dilating at the sight of my bare body before him.

"Your turn," I whispered, reaching for his belt. My fingers trembled, but whether from nerves or anticipation, I couldn't tell. All I knew was I wanted him.

His belt came undone with a soft clink of metal and soon his pants joined the rest of our discarded clothing. He was left in only his silk boxer shorts, the fabric straining against his thick and lengthy dick. I took a moment to appraise him, my eyes lingering appreciatively on the muscular sprawl of his body.

"Like what you see?"

I answered him by hooking my fingers into the waistband of his boxers and pulling them down. "Very much."

Marcus chuckled at my words, his hands reaching up to cup my face. He pulled me down for another heated kiss, our naked bodies pressing together. The sensation of our skin-to-skin contact intensified my desire.

His kisses trailed down to my nipples, lavishing attention on each one as his hand slipped between my legs. My body gave no resistance, opening to him, slick with arousal. I grunted, arching my hips to meet him as he moved his fingers in and out.

His thumb found my sensitive nub, and he circled it, making me squirm beneath him. I gripped his shoulder, nails digging into his flesh as sweet pressure built up within me. My breathing grew ragged, and I whimpered, biting my lower lip to prevent any louder sounds from escaping.

Sensing my imminent release, Marcus increased the pace of his fingers. His eyes never left mine, drinking in every gasp and moan escaping my lips. His name slipped from me in a breathless whisper as the wave crashed over me, sending me over the edge.

In one smooth motion, he flipped me over and pulled me up onto my knees, leaving my bare, round butt exposed to him.

"Magnificent," he breathed as his hands trailed from my waist down to my thighs, coaxing them apart as he settled himself behind me.

I felt the warmth of his body seeping into mine, and the thickness of him pressed against my backside. The anticipation alone made me shudder with excitement. He traced his finger along the tattoo on the back of my forearm, but to my relief didn't question it.

I heard him open a drawer from the bedside table and the rustle of a foil packet. A moment later, his latex-covered tip nudged my entrance. I moaned at the sensation, the stretch stinging but also intensely pleasurable.

His movements were slow and measured at first. But when I adjusted to his size, he picked up the rhythm. Each thrust sent ripples of pleasure coursing through me.

The feel of him moving within me was exhilarating. His hand moved to grip my hip, pulling me closer with each forward movement, while his other hand cupped and molded my breast, his thumb stroking my nipple.

The intensity of his actions sent me over the edge again and again, until I was a gasping mess beneath him, whispering his name like a mantra. He was relentless, taking me to heights of pleasure I'd never known, each climax more powerful than the last.

He shifted his weight, adjusting our bodies until he could reach down to stroke my swollen nub. The sudden contact made me jerk in surprise and pleasure. A deep thrust sent a shot of ecstasy through my body, causing me to cry out in sheer bliss.

"Breathe, Lexi," he prompted.

I could feel him throb within me, the heat and hardness of him pushing me higher, closer to the precipice.

Then all at once the coiling tension in my lower belly unraveled. A wave of pleasure so intense came over me and every cell in my body came alive. A sharp cry echoed through the room as my back arched and my body stiffened, euphoria coursing through me like lightning.

Marcus let out a low growl as I clenched around him. His grip on my hips tightened as his own climax took over.

Thrusting deeply one last time, Marcus groaned my name as he exploded. His entire body shuddered with the force of his orgasm.

We remained entwined for several moments, chests heaving and bodies slick with sweat while we rode out the aftershocks of our shared passion. When Marcus finally pulled out and collapsed next to me on the bed, I turned to face him, tucking my head into the crook of his neck.

"You okay?" he asked, reaching up to brush stray hair off my forehead.

I hummed in response, lazily drawing circles on his chest with my index finger. "More than okay," I panted.

Marcus chuckled. "That's what I like to hear."

He pressed a soft kiss on my forehead and pulled me closer to him until our naked bodies fit like two pieces of a jigsaw puzzle.

MJ

The applause and cheers still rang in my ears as I slowly gathered my legal pads and folders at the defense table. Another victory. Another life saved.

I should have been exhausted after weeks of poring over evidence, but the adrenaline coursed through me. This was what I lived for. The grind, the battle, and the victory.

Cases like this were why I became a defense attorney in the first place. The stakes had been high, but I had come through, as I always did. Failure wasn't an option for me.

Still, as much as I relished the win, something about this case gnawed at me. Siti's tearful recounting of years of abuse had stirred something deep inside me, something uncomfortable. I pushed those thoughts aside for now.

As I placed folders neatly into my briefcase, my thoughts turned inward. I felt my own pounding heart and gasping breaths as I'd stumbled upon my mother's infidelity.

I saw my father's smiling face morph into a mask of despair when my mother disappeared. I heard again the muffled sobs coming from behind my parents' bedroom door late one night when I'd visited after her abandonment.

The dark memories sunk their claws into me, as they always did after cases like this. I was glad to have won, to have helped free an innocent woman, but the costs were high.

A child without a father, a system failing many. And my own lingering disillusionment, the cynicism life had carved into my soul.

"I don't know how to thank you, Mr. Davis," Siti said over tears as she clung to my hand. "You've given me my life back!"

Looking down at her tired, careworn face, I was unexpectedly moved. Normally, I kept my distance from clients. Getting emotionally involved didn't help me do my job. But Siti was different.

Just moments ago, she had been found not guilty of a first-degree murder charge. It was a major victory, considering her unfiltered testimony to striking her husband with the skillet that ended his life.

I had convinced the jury after seventeen years of brutal emotional and physical abuse, she had acted in self-defense by protecting herself from an attack that could have killed her.

Siti threw her arms around me in a tight hug before her mother stepped in, gently leading her away. Her mother mouthed another grateful "thank you" as they left the courtroom. I watched them go, feeling satisfied not only with the outcome, but with the knowledge this win would be another step forward in my career.

As I gathered my things and headed out of the courthouse, I imagined an evening of well-deserved relaxation after weeks of tense debate and confrontation.

"Congratulations, Counselor." A familiar voice pulled me from my thoughts.

I turned to see Andrea, another attorney from my firm, fall into step beside me. Her Canadian accent gave her words a melodic lilt.

Her long brunette hair was tightly pinned up and her striking blue eyes sparkled with intelligence and something harder to ignore.

"Great work in there," she said, flashing me a grin.

Andrea was an excellent attorney, and I appreciated her praise. "Thanks, Andrea." My response was polite but brisk as we walked. I could feel her watching me, her sidelong glances growing more pointed.

"We should celebrate properly," she said, slipping her hand into the crook of my arm. There was a time when her touch might have excited me, when our shared passion for the law had sparked a real attraction. But now, it only filled me with impatience.

"I'll make dinner... your favorite pasta," she added, her fingers trailing along my arm.

Over Andrea's shoulder, I glimpsed a woman passing by whose smile reminded me fleetingly of Lexi's. Broad and warm. Andrea's eyebrows rose expectantly as she awaited my response. I pushed away the unexpected vision of Lexi, giving my head a little shake.

I knew from experience her offer of dinner came with an erotic promised after the meal was consumed. I understood this because we'd been here before.

Andrea was an attractive woman, no doubt, a bright spark in the courtroom and intimidating on the other side of a legal debate. Yet, I couldn't muster up the enthusiasm to spend time with her.

"Appreciate the offer, but I'm heading home."

Ever since my return from the States, I had withdrawn from Andrea. Resting one hand on the arm hooked through mine, I disentangled us.

Andrea's strides slowed. "We both know I'm not talking about just dinner." She stopped, facing me. "I miss you, MJ."

Her eyes were hopeful, almost vulnerable. I stopped walking. "I'm not interested."

Hurt flashed across her face, but I couldn't summon the will to care. "You used to be fun," she complained. "Now, all you do is work."

She stared up into my face, scrutinizing me. "Ever since you came back from the U.S., you've been impossible to pin down. Did something happen there?"

Memories of Lexi burned through me like wildfire. Her nails raking down my back, her laughter in the rain, the way she felt in my arms. I couldn't forget her, no matter how much I tried.

I had no desire to let Andrea in on my thoughts. "I've been preoccupied with the trial these past few months. You know how it is."

She nodded in understanding, but sidled closer. "Trials have never been a problem for you," she reminded me. "We always found ways to take your mind off work." She batted her lashes. I resisted the urge to jump away.

Andrea must have seen something in my eyes because her tone grew sharp as she asked, "Are you seeing someone else?"

I looked her over, trying not to bristle at the territorial note in her words. "Even if I was, it would be none of your business."

Her face grew red as the meaning of my declaration sank in. Her next words came out in emotional gusts.

"After all we've done together, I thought we meant something to each other. Don't you feel anything for me?" She didn't wait for my response before continuing. "I thought you and I had a future together! I thought we could be more!"

Tears glistened in her eyes, and a mottled blush spread across her cheeks. I felt bad, but not enough to back down. "You knew this was casual from the start," I said evenly. "I don't have feelings for you."

Her eyes narrowed in frustration. "You're just suspicious and defensive," she shot back. "Walking around nursing old wounds, refusing to trust anyone. Not every woman is your mother. We're not all like her."

Her words hit me like a punch, and I instinctively recoiled. I regretted ever opening up to her about my family.

Without another word, I turned and walked away. It was the safest thing I could do.

As I left, I heard her sneer, "Cowards never find love, you know."

She was probably right. But I wasn't looking for love.

The hot spray cascaded over me as I stood unmoving under the showerhead, eyes closed. Rivulets of water sluiced down the muscular contours of my back, washing away the tensions of the day.

As I reached for the soap, my thoughts drifted to the rainy night months ago. The exhilaration of the impromptu dash across the street, raindrops pelting my skin. Lexi's delighted laughter echoing in my ears over the city's noise.

I could almost feel her wet body pressed against mine as we kissed. The way her hands clasped around my neck, curves melding to the hard planes of my chest. Her delicate scent mingling with the clean petrichor of the rain.

I grabbed my erection, the memory of her touch burning through me as vivid and compelling as if she stood in the shower with me now. I remembered her teeth nipping at my lower lip, her tongue teasing a gasp from my throat. Her fingers dancing across my chest, tracing patterns on my soaked skin. The way she twined her legs around me when I hoisted her effortlessly into my arms.

The water's temperature dropped a degree or two as I leaned against the cool tile of the shower wall, dark eyes screwed shut against the onslaught of images. The soft caress of her skin against mine, sinuous and welcoming. The wild rhythm we'd danced to, hearts pounding louder than the storm.

My hand pumped faster as I recalled Lexi's gasps in my ear, little urges fanning my desire into an all-consuming blaze. I remembered how she nipped at my jawline and trailed kisses down my throat.

Groaning softly, I released under the steady stream of water. Since returning to Singapore, most of my nightly showers comprised these solitary acts of self-indulgence. Each memory of Lexi only deepening my desire.

As I rinsed off, the emptiness accompanying my post-climax clarity gnawed at me. This wasn't me. I wasn't one to pine over any woman.

Yet there was something about Lexi. Something in the way her lips moved when she spoke. Something in the twinkle of her eyes when she laughed.

The memory of her haunted my every waking moment, and even my dreams. Those dreams brought me to this state; a man caught between his desires for a woman and his need to forget her.

As I stepped out of the shower, I looked at my reflection in the mirror and noticed a new tiredness in my eyes. My mind wandered back to Valentine's night again, but I shook my head, forcefully discarding the thought.

Enough was enough. I grabbed the fluffy towel from its rack, wrapping it around my waist. Exiting the bathroom, I crossed the spacious bedroom and slumped onto the edge of the bed.

For the past year, my mind had been wandering, questioning the comfortable life I'd built here in Singapore. I'd achieved everything I set out to. Career, prestige, more money than I would spend. On paper, my life was perfect. But it lacked a deeper meaning.

My personal phone pinged, bringing my mind back to the present. The text was from my brother-in-law, prince Nassir Al-Qadir. Nassir's message was succinct as usual.

> Your sister misses you.

Nassir wasn't the type to waste his time being wordy.

I smiled, tapping out an answer quickly.

> I miss her too. Been busy. Huge case.

> I heard. Congrats.

I shook my head in amusement. Nassir and Trina lived on a luxury-yacht — *Inescapable* — sailing the world and already the news of my victory had filtered to my brother-in-law.

I shouldn't be surprised. The man kept tabs on his in-laws. Safety and security reasons, he'd claimed. Three little dots bobbed on the screen, and then more of Nassir's words appeared.

> Your father and sister are joining Trina on the yacht in a few weeks. I want you to join them. Having Trina's entire family and closest friends on the yacht is one of my anniversary gifts to her. When should I expect you there?

A vacation? The very idea grated against my work-focused mind. My caseloads wouldn't wait for me, and I had clients who depended on me. But then again... maybe that was the problem.

I had been running nonstop for years and it was catching up to me. My mind was sharp, but my body was tired. And if I wanted to keep pursuing my goals, I needed to be at my best. Maybe a break wouldn't be such a bad idea after all.

My sisters and father would be thrilled to have me there. They constantly accused me of not visiting enough. The last time I was in Valleyfield was two Christmases ago. It had been the first time I met my nephew, Lucas, Hazel's son. The boy was four years old now.

I saw Trina last summer because Nassir had a business engagement in Singapore and brought his family along. Trina had invited me to lunch, and I'd met Trina's newborn son, Javed, for the first time.

I could almost hear the rolling waves of the ocean and smell the salty ocean air. My heart yearned for a small pocket of peace with my family.

With a sigh, I stomped over to the large window overlooking the twinkling Singapore skyline. The city always felt alive, pulsing with restless energy.

Thoughts of Lexi crept in again, her laughter echoing in my mind. Maybe a change of scenery was exactly what I needed to shake her from my thoughts. To move forward.

I turned away from the window and saw the stack of papers strewn across my bedside table.

Sorry man. Can't make it. Trina'll understand.

It wasn't a suggestion.

I'm willing to use force to get you here if necessary.

A low chuckle escaped me when I imagined burly bodyguards sneaking into my apartment in the middle of the night, bundling me up and whisking me away to some secret helipad. It almost made me want to resist to see how far Nassir would take this.

Nassir's expectation for me to drop everything didn't rankle as much as it should. I knew the man loved my sister deeply and wanted her happiness.

The question now left was whether I could detach myself from my work-obsessed life for a while. Could I put aside the demands of my career to enjoy my family, the sea, and some relaxation?

You win.

I typed and send the message.

A response came in almost immediately.

You made the right choice. I'll have a plane ready for you.

Lexi

"**A**re you sure I'm not intruding?" I asked in a small voice. No matter how hard I tried, I couldn't quite believe I was standing on a yacht docked at Marina Grande in Capri. And not just any yacht: the *Inescapable*, the long-term home of an Arabian prince and his queen.

It was the largest and most luxurious vessel I'd ever seen. The interior was breathtaking, with plush furniture, gleaming ornate lighting, and state-of-the-art technology.

But the deck we were lounging on? It was something else entirely. It had everything—a bar, a helipad, even pools. This was the largest of three decks, scattered with chairs and loungers, perfect for relaxing in the sun.

Trina Al-Qadir, my hostess, laughed warmly. "That's the second time you've asked me since this morning," she said, smiling. "But I get it. I suffer from imposter syndrome, too." She reached over from her lounger and gave my sunscreen-slicked arm a reassuring pat. "You're welcome here. No, you're not intruding. But if you ask again, I might just throw you overboard."

"And I'll help her do it," Kneshel chimed in from the other side of me, lounging in a bikini and colorful wrap. She was one of Trina's best friends, and the reason I was on this trip. Kneshel had lived on this vessel for a time and delivered both of Trina's babies.

I smiled from one to the other, still unable to keep my mind from boggling at my new reality, but not daring to express my wonderment once more. It was early June, with summer temperatures rising. I was embarking on the vacation of a lifetime. This was my first trip out of Valleyfield and Montrose.

It was a gathering of family and friends, as Trina's sisters, Hazel and Amy, relaxed on nearby loungers swirling ice in their bottomless daiquiri glasses and laughing amongst themselves. Trina's other best friends, Marlowe and Joy, were also present, as were Trina's dad and his girlfriend, but they were resting in their cabin. Trina's husband Nassir was in his home country for business, leaving the yacht decked with security personnel.

I gazed out at the shimmering blue sea surrounding us. The salty tang of the ocean mingled with the sweet scent of coconut oil warming on sun-kissed skin. A light breeze ruffled my braids as it swept over the spacious deck.

Overhead, gulls cried out as they circled and dove around the vessel. The sun glinted off their white wings before they plunged into the cerulean water in search of food. I resisted the urge to join them, longing to slip into the cool waves.

Instead, I sank into the plush cushion of the deck chair, grateful for the shade provided by the brightly striped umbrella overhead. The other women's voices washed over me, their laughter twining together with the melodic accents of the waiting staff as they delivered an endless array of colorful cocktails and frosty drinks.

My gaze drifted over the expanse of polished white deck, taking in the gleaming hot tub, the infinity pool with its dazzling view of sea meeting sky, and the many sun-soaked nooks perfect for lounging with a book or quiet conversation.

It was remarkable to think how far Trina had come. She was an ordinary girl from Valleyfield, the daughter of a mechanic and a bookkeeper, now living in such luxury. I wondered how she felt about it all.

Did the extravagance ever overwhelm her, or had she grown accustomed to this life? Knowing Trina, she probably handled it with grace, just like everything else. But I couldn't help but think how surreal it must be for her sometimes, to look around and see herself surrounded by such wealth.

Trina tapped on her glass with a spoon. "Okay, ladies, listen up!"

It took a few seconds for the women to tear their attention away from what they were doing and turn in Trina's direction. When Trina had their attention, her voice rang out with excitement. "I just wanted you guys to know how much it means to me to have you here. Considering how busy our lives are—"

"Not all of us!" Hazel teased. "You get to sip cocktails by the pool every day!"

Trina shushed her sister and continued. "I know I don't go home as often as I should, and video-calling you is nice, but nothing like having you all here. So welcome." She went on with a mischievous smile. "I've created an itinerary."

"Itinerary!" Marlowe faked a groan. "What's this? Our senior class trip?"

Trina flashed a talk-to-the-hand gesture. "Hush. You know you're gonna love it because it's a party-till-you-drop itinerary. And here's what's on it." She made a big show of clearing her throat and began. "First, for the kids, I've arranged activities on and off the yacht."

All the mommies — every woman except me — straightened up and listened.

"My nanny, Khadija, is an expert in early childhood development and for the duration of this trip, I've hired three other well-trained child sitters. We have a few arts and crafts activities planned as well as baking and picnicking."

"Lucas will love that," Hazel murmured.

"There's going to be daily exercise classes," Trina said.

"For the kids or us?" Joy wanted to know.

The other women chuckled, and Trina smiled at her. "Both. It will be kid-inclusive sessions." She added. "There will also be shopping, shopping, more shopping, high tea, dance parties, and maybe some more shopping."

"I just want to lounge around the pool all day," Amy said with a dramatic sigh, stretching her legs out in front of her. "While the nanny cares for Aurelia. Whoever came up with the term terrible twos never lied!"

Marlowe let out a snort. "It doesn't get better when they turn three... Four is the sweet spot."

Hazel and Trina nodded their heads in agreement.

"Between the kids and Trina's non-stop itinerary, I don't think our toddlers will find the time to show their asses," Hazel said.

"It's a vacation, not a death march," Trina objected. "You all are free to do as you want. There is a massage therapist on board and a spa for those who want a break."

"Remember Trina's bachelorette party?" Joy chuckled. "My feet have never forgiven me."

"This trip will be nothing like my bachelorette," Trina insisted. "Right, Kneshel?"

Kneshel nearly choked on her drink. "Well… at least there are no treasure hunts."

"Not you too!" Trina exclaimed.

"Hey, we're just giving you a hard time," Marlowe said, patting Trina's leg affectionately. "We know you want us all to have a good time."

"And we will," Kneshel assured her. "Now stop pouting and come sit."

"I've died and gone to heaven," Amy murmured after taking a deep sip from her custom cocktail. "This is the nectar of the gods."

"I can't wait till it gets dark and the stars come out," Hazel said.

The other women agreed, having all experienced nighttime on the yacht. I looked around at the smiling, cheerful, content women and couldn't help but feel my spirit dip. Everyone belonged here except me.

All of them were married, and from the snippets of conversation during the private flight and since our arrival, it seemed they were all in happy relationships. Each had kids, and they had brought them along for this vacation. This girls' trip was an annual tradition for the group.

It was Trina's way of keeping her closest friends and their families connected. I was relieved none of the husbands had joined, as their presence would have only made my own loneliness more pronounced and unbearable.

I smiled, hoping no one noticed how despondent I really felt. My original plans for this vacation had been to help Ben take care of his terminally ill mother.

But when Kneshel heard about it, she begged me to come with her instead, promising two weeks of much-needed relaxation. I eventually agreed, especially after both Ben and Aunt Sheryl insisted I take this once-in-a-lifetime opportunity.

It didn't stop my thoughts from to Aunt Sheryl, though. Was she comfortable? Was Ben and Tiffany managing okay without me?

Aunt Sheryl had always been there for me, and now she was unwell. It felt wrong to be so far away. I should be there to help, to make her laugh, to hold her hand.

But Tiffany had promised she'd call if anything changed... Still, I couldn't shake the feeling I should be doing more.

As if sensing my thoughts, Kneshel leaned toward me, her bare arm brushing against mine. "I'm looking forward to spending some girl time with you."

Trina overheard and raised her glass. "To a great time and making this year's trip unforgettable!"

The others quickly followed suit, clinking their glasses with enthusiasm. "Hear, hear!"

Their attention soon drifted back to their own conversations, and I found myself on the sidelines again. I smiled tightly and took a small sip of my cocktail as bursts of laughter erupted from the other loungers. Hazel and Joy were practically falling over, their wide-brimmed hats tilting precariously as they laughed at something Amy had said.

Nearby, Trina and Marlowe were deep into a discussion about their high school days, with Kneshel chiming in occasionally about her own teenage years. Their champagne flutes clinked together after each amusing story.

I shifted on my lounger, crossing my legs beneath my sundress, and pressed my cold, condensation-covered glass against my thigh.

I listened wistfully to the easy rhythm of their voices, so comfortable with one another.

They made a few attempts to include me, asking questions or directing comments my way. I responded, trying to engage, but it was hard to fully immerse myself in their world. Despite my efforts, I kept drifting back to the edges, feeling like an outsider.

I watched Trina's gaze flick toward the stairway, her smile growing wider with each glance. I didn't ask what she was looking at. It wasn't my place to pry.

Kneshel also noticed Trina's preoccupation and paused mid-story. "What's going on?" she asked, squinting against the sun as she followed Trina's gaze.

"A surprise for Hazel," Trina whispered, turning her attention back to the group.

Marlowe leaned in, intrigued. "Ooh, a surprise? What kind of surprise?" She playfully nudged Trina. "Come on, spill!"

Kneshel's eyes lit up. "Is Isaac coming?" she asked excitedly. Isaac Wesson was Hazel's husband and Trina's biological brother.

"Shh!" Trina pressed a finger to her lips, her eyes sparkling with mischief. She glanced over at Hazel, who was still engrossed in conversation with Joy and Amy, completely unaware. With a reluctant smile, Trina leaned in and whispered, "Okay, okay. M—"

Before she could finish, a deep voice interrupted, cutting through the moment and freezing me in place.

"You ladies look like you're having a great time."

The voice brought my world to a standstill. My heart lurched.

I knew that voice all too well. It belonged to the man who had whispered in my ear during moments of passion, the man who had lingered in my thoughts for months after that night.

But I couldn't let myself get carried away. I had to stay grounded, logical.

"MJ!" Hazel sprang to her feet, rushing across the deck with her arms wide open, squealing like a child. "What are you doing here?" She didn't wait for his response before turning to Trina with mock indignation. "Why didn't you tell me our brother was coming?"

Trina waved off the question with a casual flick of her wrist, the ornate bangles on her arm tinkling. "I didn't know he was coming until he landed on the helipad last night. We decided to surprise you and Dad."

Hazel's face lit up with a wide smile, the corners of her eyes crinkling. "I'm guessing this was Nassir's idea." She clung to Marcus, practically bouncing on her toes. "Wait until Lucas finds out his uncle is here!"

Marcus smiled down at his sister, the late afternoon sun reflecting off his sunglasses. "I stopped by the playroom before coming up. Lucas and I had a nice, long visit."

"I wondered what was keeping you," Trina said, glancing at him.

Marcus turned to her, chuckling. "Dad's down there now wearing a pink feather boa and a princess crown while he and the kids stage an elaborate tea party."

Watching the family reunion unfold, I wished I could disappear. How long before Marcus noticed the rest of us? Before he noticed me?

What would he do when he saw me? Would he acknowledge me or pretend we were strangers? And if he did react, would it be anger, resentment... disgust?

I stifled a groan, barely keeping it from escaping. Why had I agreed to come on this trip? Marcus wasn't here for a quick hello.

His presence in the middle of the Tyrrhenian Sea meant he was here for the full family gathering.

I should've trusted my instincts. I didn't belong here. I should've been spending what might be Aunt Sheryl's last days with her, not vacationing on a yacht with Marcus's family. Why had I ever thought this was a good idea?

Shrinking into the background, I pulled my shoulders in and sank lower into my seat, hoping to become invisible. My heart pounded as Marcus finished chatting with his sisters and turned his attention to the other women, asking about their husbands. His deep voice sent a flare of heat through my veins.

I couldn't stop staring at him. His tall, broad frame and muscular arms had once held me possessively. The memory of my reckless desire mocked me now.

Pressing my thighs together under the table, I felt warmth pooling in my belly at the thought of him between them. The phantom sensation made me shiver, even in the Tyrrhenian heat.

One by one, Marcus engaged the women, charming them with ease. I could see how much they liked him by the way they smiled and laughed. With each conversation, the moment I dreaded drew closer.

I silently cursed myself for the wanton thoughts racing through my mind. How could I still crave a man who probably hated me for slipping away like a thief in the night? I couldn't let him see how deeply he affected me, how easily his presence could unravel me.

Hazel's voice broke through my spiraling thoughts. "Come on, MJ, sit down! We have so much to catch up on. We'll get a steward to bring you a drink."

"Yeah," Trina agreed, reaching for the intercom to call the staff. "What are you having? I'll order it."

Marcus pulled out a chair with a satisfied grunt. "I don't mind a drink. I'm still jet—"

His words cut off abruptly, his eyes widening as they landed on me.

MJ

I wasn't prepared to see her.

The second my eyes landed on her, everything around me shifted, as if the ground beneath my feet had suddenly changed. Colors blurred and sounds faded as my eyes drank in the sight of her.

My mind couldn't process it fast enough. One moment, I was easing into the familiar rhythm of sibling repartee, the next, I was staring at the woman who'd disappeared from my bed without a word.

My gaze to swept her length, noting a light, colorful beach wrap over a bright pink bikini. It looked positively delectable against the brown of her skin.

Her hair was freshly braided, probably done specially for the trip. The diamond nose ring and eyebrow stud I remembered had been replaced with simple steel ones.

I wanted her.

The desire rivaled the hunger I'd experienced the night I'd met her. And it wasn't fair.

I'd struggled over the past months to forget her, and I'd almost succeeded. She had become a haunting memory in the peripheries of my mind, and here she was again, in the flesh, ready to provoke and disturb my peace.

When I finally spoke, my voice came out rougher than I intended. "What are you doing here?"

"You two know each other?" Trina asked.

I forced myself to look away from Lexi and turned to my sister. "We've met."

Kneshel chimed in. "Montrose, right? Valentine's Day?"

Lexi nodded, clearly uncomfortable. She shifted in her seat, her fingers anxiously smoothing the cocktail napkin in front of her.

Hazel's accusatory question interrupted my thoughts. "You were in Montrose?"

Great. I held up my hands to placate Hazel before I suffered her ire. "It was for one night."

"But still," Hazel pressed. "You could've mentioned it!"

Before I could respond, I heard the scrape of a chair. Lexi stood, pushing her half-finished drink aside. "I think I'll go lie down for a bit," she mumbled, already retreating.

As if on cue, the other women also rose, probably sensing a family discussion was about to begin. I wanted to call out to Lexi, ask her to stay, but I didn't. Instead, I contented myself with watching the perfect view of her swaying hips and irresistible, round ass as she walked away.

She didn't glance back, leaving me with a bittersweet longing. It was hard to believe we were stuck on the same yacht for the next two weeks after convincing myself I'd never see her again.

Was this some kind of sign? Should I pursue something with her while we were both here?

The thought of casual hookups during the trip was tempting. Our connection felt just as intense as it had before. Her flushed face and avoidance of eye contact told me she hadn't forgotten either. What harm could come from a little fun?

Plenty, said the rational part of me. This was supposed to be a family vacation. I was here for my sisters and our father, not to chase after a woman who was a guest of my sister. Was I losing my mind?

Maybe, came the answer. But the thought of feeling Lexi's body against mine again, hearing her soft sighs and moans, was almost too much to resist.

"Hey!" Hazel snapped her fingers in front of my face, pulling me back to reality. "Whatever planet you're on, come back to earth."

Trina wasn't far behind, her expression equally annoyed. "Yeah, we want answers!"

I shook off thoughts of Lexi and focused on my sisters. Whenever they teamed up against me, I was in trouble. "I barely had time to sleep, let alone call my dear meddling sisters."

Hazel swatted my arm. "Meddling? I prefer the term caring."

"And protective," Trina added. "We want to know what's going on in your life."

"And meet all your lady friends," Hazel said with an exaggerated wink. "Are you seeing anyone?"

I rolled my eyes. "You two are ridiculous."

"We're related to you, so that makes sense," Trina quipped.

I sighed, letting the sea breeze soothe my thoughts as I gazed out at the endless blue horizon. "I went to Montrose for a job interview," I began, meeting their expectant stares. "I didn't mention it because I wasn't sure how it would go, and I didn't want to get your hopes up."

Trina's eyes widened. "You're thinking of moving back to the States?"

"What job?" Hazel asked. "Where? In Montrose? Is it at a law firm?"

I shook my head. "It was a teaching position. Montrose University was looking for a law professor. I thought I fit their requirements, so I applied."

"Awesome!" Hazel squealed, her earlier annoyance vanishing at the prospect of having me back in town. "When do you start?"

"They offered it to someone else, I think."

"What?" Hazel looked stunned. "Are they insane?"

Trina wasn't any happier. "Did you include your full résumé? Do they know everything you've achieved?"

I smiled. "I know how to write a solid CV, Trina. The interview went really well."

"Then they're idiots," she declared.

"Total dumbasses," Hazel added.

"Second-rate college—"

"They clearly don't recognize talent—"

"They'll regret it," Trina muttered darkly. "Just wait."

I laughed. "You sound like you're about to cast a curse on them."

"Not a curse," she said, half-serious. "But maybe Nassir can purchase the university."

I wasn't entirely sure she was joking, so I placed my hands over hers. "Please don't buy a university for me. I'm fine with their decision." Disappointed, sure, but sometimes that's how life goes. I had already come to terms with it.

Hazel, however, was eyeing me carefully. "So... does this mean you won't be moving back anytime soon?"

"Well, I'm also considering an offer from a college in New York."

Both my sisters gasped. "You're moving to New York *now*? After we left and begged you to come when we lived there? That's not fair!"

I raised a hand to calm them. "Nothing's decided yet."

There was no need to mention the exhaustion of living abroad or my desire to find a place in the U.S. wherever that might be. The conversation had already stirred enough emotions for one day.

Shifting focus, I suggested we head below deck to visit the kids. They happily agreed, and for the next couple of hours, I was completely absorbed in playing with my niece and nephews as they excitedly showed me their toys and dragged me around the play area. For a while, I managed to forget those arresting dark-brown eyes.

Once the nannies took the children for their naps, I found myself alone again. Needing a distraction, I headed to the main pool, stripped down, and dove in. The cool water was a welcome relief in the growing heat of the afternoon sun, now well past its peak.

I swam in long, steady strokes, counting laps in my head, letting my mind slip into a meditative rhythm. But with my guard down, thoughts of Lexi crept back in. Every time I surfaced for air, I found myself scanning the deck, wondering if I'd see her standing there, her legs reflected in the water's rippling surface.

Where the hell was she? This ship was massive, but I wasn't about to let that stop me. I couldn't just sit here and wonder. I needed to find her, talk to her, figure out what the hell was going on.

The thought of her avoiding me, hiding away in her cabin, made my blood heat. If she thought she could avoid me for two weeks, she was dead wrong.

Later, gathered around the banquet table for supper, the women chattered around me, but Lexi was nowhere to be seen. Kneshel mentioned she'd decided to have her meal in her room.

"I hope she's not still feeling like an outsider," said Trina.

Hazel reassured her, "We'll just have to work harder to make her feel welcome."

I stayed quiet, knowing full well the real reason for Lexi's absence: my presence at the table. But what did her avoidance mean? Was it a good sign or a bad one?

After dinner, the women stayed on the upper deck, sipping cocktails and laughing as they gazed out at the dark sea, illuminated only by a sliver of moonlight. I joined in the conversation, turning on the charm and genuinely enjoying myself. For a couple of hours, I found that the best remedy for my unease was talking.

As we chatted, my eyes kept drifting around the deck. Who was I looking for?

I already knew the answer. The woman who had occupied far too many of my thoughts over the past few months.

Ridiculous.

What were the odds of running into her here, of all places? I forced myself to stay focused on the conversation, pushing away the memory of Lexi's lips, the warmth of her skin under my hands...

Enough. That was in the past. But as I told myself to move on, a nagging voice reminded me, *she's here. You'll see her again.*

One by one, the women began heading to their cabins, mentioning calls to their husbands before bed. My sisters were the last to leave, hugging me tightly and reminding me how happy they were to have me here. After they left, I lingered on the deck, staring out at the vast, black ocean under the stars.

Footsteps approached. I turned to see Robyn, my father's girl-friend. "Beautiful night, isn't it?" Robyn said, joining me at the railing.

I nodded.

She studied me more closely. "You seem lost in thought. Do you want me to leave?"

I shook my head, offering a half-hearted smile. "No, I could do with the company, actually." I took a drink from my glass, the cool bourbon burning a trail down my throat.

Robyn leaned on the railing next to me, her gaze following mine out into the inky expanse of the sea. "Something bothering you?" She asked after a moment's silence.

I hesitated before sighing heavily. "More like someone."

Her eyebrows shot up in surprise. "Oh? Anyone we know?"

I shook my head. I wasn't prepared to tell anyone about Lexi.

Robyn studied me for a moment before nodding, seemingly satisfied with my response. "Well," she started, leaning back against the railing and crossing her arms over her chest. "She must be something special if she's got you out here contemplating."

I could only offer a chuckle in response. "You have no idea."

Time stretched between us, broken only by the gentle sound of waves lapping against the yacht. After a few moments, Robyn spoke, her voice softer.

"You know, MJ," she said, "life has a funny way of working things out."

I turned to her.

"In my experience," she continued, "people sometimes come into our lives when we least expect it and they change everything."

"Is that what happened with you and Dad?" I asked, my tone balancing between humor and curiosity.

Robyn chuckled, her brown eyes sparkling with a distant memory. "You could say that. Who knew a junky car would lead me to my soulmate at forty-five?"

I thought about the new light in my father's eyes since he began dating Robyn, the way he laughed more freely, and suddenly I understood what she meant.

"You're saying... I should just let it happen?" I ventured, looking at her with uncertainty.

Robyn nodded, placing a comforting hand on my arm. "Stop overthinking," she said. "And trust that things will work out as they should."

I considered her words as I stared out into the dark ocean again. After a while, Robyn patted my arm before excusing herself for the night, leaving me alone with my thoughts.

Staring at the moon's reflection dancing on the dark surface of the ocean, the jet lag set in. I trudged to my cabin, undressed, and got into bed.

I laid with my hands interlaced behind my head, staring up at the ceiling. The moon drifted from one side of the vessel to the other, and still I found no respite.

Cursing in frustration, I threw off the light covers, swung my feet over the side of the bed, and stood. Maybe a walk would help relax me. There was a small jogging track up top, but it wasn't where my feet led me.

Instead, I treaded lightly down to the lower deck, looking over my shoulder as I did. Was anyone following my movements?

Every step I took, every turn down the hallway, I knew where I was going. Lexi's door.

I couldn't let her hide from me. I wasn't the type to let things go unresolved, and I wasn't about to start now.

During dinner, Trina had given her staff instructions as to which cabin to deliver Lexi's food. I'd pocketed her room number in my memory. Of course, my restless spirit had led me here. Where else would I possibly end up tonight?

When I reached her cabin, I didn't hesitate. My hand moved to the doorknob, ready to confront her head-on.

"What are you doing?" someone demanded from behind me, just as I turned the doorknob.

Lexi

I froze, my mind racing to process the sight of Marcus—clad in loose gray sweatpants and a white t-shirt outlining the contours of his well-built torso—standing at my door. What was he doing here? Of all the times and places...

My first instinct was to panic, but I forced myself to breathe. Think. This wasn't just some chance encounter. He came here for a reason.

"What are you doing here?" I breathed out, my gaze lingering momentarily on the soft cotton that did little to conceal the vitality it covered.

"Lexi," Marcus stammered out my name, making it sound like a plea, an apology, or possibly both. His obsidian-black eyes met mine. "I had to see you." His voice was low but clear, cutting through the tension.

"Why?" My voice was sharper than I intended. The ease with which he had disrupted my calm was infuriating.

I straightened my back and squared my shoulders, hoping to come across as intimidating, even though it was ridiculous. He was a foot taller and at least eighty pounds heavier than me.

I watched as another wave of guilt flushed across his face. He let go of the doorknob and let his hand fall to his side. "We need to talk."

"There's nothing to talk about," I deadpanned.

"I disag—" he began.

There was the metallic thud of footsteps on the deck and I felt a moment of panic. Maybe it was the guards on patrol… or maybe it was one of the other guests. If we were found outside my cabin at this hour, there would be many uncomfortable questions.

Acting swiftly, I moved past Marcus, opened my cabin door, and entered. He followed closely behind me, shutting the door behind him. The footsteps faded and were soon replaced by the now-familiar hum of the engines and the lapping of the water on the hull way below.

The man I'd been steadfastly avoiding was now inside my cabin.

Taking a deep exhale, I turned to face Marcus in the dim light of the cabin. His massive frame filled most of the door space, making the room feel much smaller than it was. I crossed my arms across my chest and took a step back.

Rubbing his strong jawline with his fingers, Marcus glanced around the cabin. His eyes finally rested on the king-sized bed, whose white sheets were tossed and rumpled.

"Okay," I began, trying to keep my voice steady. "What do you want to discuss?"

"Are you afraid of me?" he asked.

He took a step closer. Tentatively, rather than threateningly, as if testing to see whether I would flee. I was immediately overwhelmed by an electric thrill as my body registered his proximity and the sheer power of his presence.

"Lexi?"

"I'm not." I averted my gaze from his face and shook my head vehemently.

Afraid of him? Hell, no. But totally afraid of what I might allow him to do.

To both my horror and my delight, he stepped closer, his presence swallowing the small space between us. I instinctively backed up, but the bed was behind me, leaving nowhere to go.

He knew it, too. There was a challenge in his eyes, daring me to push him away, but I couldn't. His body blocked any escape, his nearness making it clear that he wasn't leaving until he got what he came for.

Marcus' thumb brushed my lower lip, sending sparks dancing across my skin. There was nothing tentative about him. Each movement, each touch, was deliberate, as if he knew exactly how to unravel me with the smallest gesture.

When I finally dared meet his gaze, the raw hunger in his dark eyes stole my breath. Memories rose like a tidal wave, drowning my senses. Our bodies intertwined on that too-small hotel bed, my gasps and pleas mingling with his low groans. His large hands gripping my backside, fingers digging into supple flesh as he plowed into me.

My throat went dry. Marcus' chuckle reverberated through me. "You're thinking about how good we feel together," he murmured, his voice dripping with certainty.

It wasn't a question. He leaned closer, his breath hot against my skin, daring me to deny it.

"No." I could still feel the imprint of his body on mine, the lingering caress of his hands.

He chuckled again, the rich sound sending tingles to my core. He saw through my resistance, past my words, straight to the desire I was trying hard to ignore. And he didn't hesitate to exploit. His eyes gleamed with a confidence making it clear he wouldn't leave until I gave in.

"I was thinking of my dogs, and wondering how they're getting along with the sitter," I lied.

As if I could think of anything but his hard muscles enveloping me, his skillful hands awakening nerve endings I didn't know existed. I shivered despite the warmth of the cabin, acutely aware of his towering presence.

"Kung and Fu, right?" He sounded amused, suggesting he saw right through my flimsy deflection. "How are they?"

"Fine," I muttered ungraciously, despite my amazement at his remembering their names after only being told once.

I hadn't thought of Kung and Fu once since learning of Marcus' presence on the yacht. Poor things were probably missing me terribly.

I made a mental note to FaceTime Ben first thing in the morning and check on them. He had generously offered to pup-sit while I was away, but my sweet fur babies had never been apart from me this long before. I hoped they were faring okay without their mama.

"You left without saying goodbye." There was more puzzlement and hurt in the statement than anger.

"You didn't come after me." But even as I said it, I knew how stupid it sounded.

He sighed gustily, as if he was contemplating taking my accusation head-on, but dismissed the idea. "Let's not talk about the past. I want to talk about the now."

"Now?" I queried, curious despite myself.

"Here we are," he explained, "thrown into each other's company for the next two weeks." His mouth curved a little. "I want to make the most of it."

"This is your sister's home," I reminded him.

"I know," he answered.

"Kneshel invited me here and your sister welcomed me. What would your sisters think of me if they found out I was...uh..." I was too embarrassed to complete the thought.

"If they found out you were... what, Lexi?" he pressed, his voice dropping an octave lower, caressing my name in a way that made my guts flip. His gaze was unwavering, ensnaring me like the spell woven by a gifted sorcerer.

I swallowed, my heart pounding like a runaway mule. "If they found out I was...involved with you," I said, my voice barely above a whisper.

Marcus's hands slid under my shirt, caressing the sensitive skin of my lower back. I shuddered at the contact, my traitorous body arching closer even as warning bells went off in my mind.

"We shouldn't," I managed, my voice weak against the certainty in his eyes.

But Marcus didn't pull back. He wasn't moved by my words. If anything, they spurred him on. He was relentless, undeterred by my half-hearted protest..

"We will." His voice was a promise, not a question.

He was staring down at my mouth as if he wanted to devour them. *Stop*, I warned myself, as the desire to kiss him grew inside me, threatening to become uncontrollable.

"We can't," I objected, though my racing heart knew I was paying lip service to propriety.

"Says who?" he said huskily, the citrus scent of his skin enveloping me.

He was closer now, and then there was no space between us. His hard body was pressed against my soft curves and I had to tilt my head back to see his face.

I should tell him to leave. Any rational person would stop this before it went any further.

But when his lips found mine, all my carefully constructed defenses crumbled. His kiss was an assault, a claim of ownership making me whimper against his mouth. I was overwhelmed, unable to think or react. My hands found his hair, tugging him closer as our tongues met in a heated dance.

When he raised his lips, I cried in protest, grabbing his head and pulling him back to me. Instead of reclaiming my lips, he trailed kisses along my face, down my chin, to my throat. Down lower to my shoulder, pushing aside the collar of my shirt to grant him more access.

Then the room was tilting...no, wait, I was tilting as he pushed me backward onto the bed. At his urging, I shimmied my hips as I scooted backward until only my lower legs hanged off the edge of the bed.

"Perfect," Marcus mumbled, and set about pulling and tugging until my leggings were down around my ankles. He peeled them off and threw them to the floor, and immediately took on the delightful task of treating my thin cotton panties the same way.

Marcus then kneeled between my knees, his gaze riveted to the apex of my thighs. He dragged his tongue across his lips.

But whether it was a warning or a promise, I didn't know. He then looked up, directly into my eyes, and grinned.

"You do not know how long I've waited to taste your sweetness again," he confessed in a low whisper.

Then, without another word, lowered his face and buried it between my thighs.

I gasped as his warm tongue swiped over my clitoris. My hands instinctively cradled his head.

My world shifted again as his hot mouth began exploring, teasing me in a way no other man had ever done. His powerful hands held me firm, his thumbs stroking the sensitive skin of my inner thighs. It was an overwhelming assault on my senses, a flood of emotion and sensation that left me dizzy, struggling for breath.

I tilted my pelvis to give him the right angle for pleasurable contact, and wrapped my legs around his head, locking him there. Taking him prisoner.

I writhed beneath him, the intensity of his touch pushing me towards a precipice I knew there was no coming back from. With every flick of his tongue, every slow drag of his lips against sensitive skin, I felt myself spiraling closer to the edge. I whimpered, clutching at him as though he were the only thing grounding me in this whirlwind of sensation.

I whipped my head from side to side, bursting with incandescent energy. I was right there... close to the edge...

A light knock sounded from my cabin door.

My heart pounded against my rib cage like a trapped bird. I tried to push Marcus off me again, but his grip was iron-clad.

"We have to stop," I hissed.

Instead of letting me up, he grabbed my ass tighter, fingers burrowing into my flesh. Marcus was larger, stronger, and I couldn't budge.

"I have you right where I want you," he murmured.

"There's someone..." I whispered.

"I don't give a fuck," he grumbled, and I whimpered as his tongue flicked my sensitive nub, electrifying my senses.

"Lexi?" It was Kneshel's voice, querying, curious. "You okay?"

I clenched my teeth together to suppress a moan as Marcus continued with his tantalizing ministrations. "Uh..." I panted. I tried again. "Yes."

"I heard noises, and I was wondering if you were sick."

Had my moans of pleasure really sounded to a qualified doctor like someone being sick? I gave Marcus a hard push, but he remained immovable, his face buried between my thighs.

"Marcus," I whispered, the warning clear in my voice.

He ignored me though, his tongue continuing its torturous trail up and down my sensitive folds as if we had all the time in the world.

My scrambled brain struggled to find a suitable lie. "It's the T.V. Sorry if it's too loud."

Kneshel seemed to buy my story. "You didn't join us for dinner. Wanted to make sure everything's okay."

"I'm... fine," I said weakly, while Marcus dove in even deeper.

Each flicker of his tongue set off fireworks in me that left me teetering on the brink of insanity.

"I'll try... to keep it down," I promised, struggling to hold my voice steady.

Kneshel seemed mollified. "Goodnight."

Then I was teetering on the brink of ecstasy. His name slipped from my lips in a breathy plea as warmth pooled in the pit of my stomach. He responded by deepening the rhythm and intensity of his exploration, eliciting a shuddering sigh from deep within me.

It was dizzying, all-consuming, the world spinning and reforming as waves upon waves of pleasure crashed over me. It took all of Marcus's strength to keep me from falling off the bed. I shoved my fist into my mouth to prevent myself from screaming, and still the man didn't let up.

After what felt like an eternity, he finally emerged from between my legs. I was still panting heavily, my body twitching from the aftershock of one of the most intense orgasms I'd ever experienced. He slid up the length of me, his strong physique pressing against my pliant form. His gaze bore into mine, full of lust.

"That was close," he observed. "You'll have to be more quiet next time."

My rational mind snapped back into place at his words, and the weight of what I'd done settled over me like a heavy blanket. I'd let my emotions override my common sense. It was the very thing I'd promised myself I wouldn't do.

How had I let this happen? I had always prided myself on being in control, on thinking things through. But with Marcus... I'd lost that control.

Staggering to my feet, I hauled him up as well and pointed to the door. "There won't be a next time," I informed him firmly.

"There won't?" he asked with a note of humorous taunting in his voice.

"No," I insisted firmly, my words serving to convince myself as much as him. "There won't. Now," I held open the door and pointed. "Out."

"I'll leave," he said, his voice low and filled with intent. His eyes never left mine, and the way he said it made it clear this wasn't the end. "But don't think for a second this is over." His lips curved into a knowing smile, as if he'd already won.

I closed the door after he left and breathed a sigh of relief. Deep down, I knew he was right. This was far from over.

MJ

I was buttering toast for my nephew the next morning when Lexi joined us. She moved gracefully, her knitted beach dress billowing around her, shrouding my full view of the purple bikini she wore underneath.

After greeting the group, Lexi collected some fruit and made herself a coffee. I watched as she added cream and sugar, her bottom jiggling with her movements.

My grip on the butter knife tightened. I ached to pull her into my arms, to feel her soft curves pressed against me once more, yet frustration simmered at her polite smiles and demure chatter. Her composure revealed none of the fiery passion she showed in my arms the previous night and contrasted with my restlessness.

This wasn't who I was. Marcus Davis Jr, always self-possessed, passionately pursuing career over women.

Yet, something about Lexi obliterated my disciplined control. Her curvy body called to a primal part of me, hungry for softness, warmth, intimacy. But it was more than physical longing.

It was something beyond the realms of simple desire or lust, something profound. A connection I found both terrifying and exhilarating.

As I watched her laugh at something Hazel said, her eyes sparkling with genuine warmth, I felt a fresh wave of longing wash over me. I yearned to know her thoughts, her dreams, to understand what made her smile and what brought tears to her beautiful eyes.

I handed my nephew the toast and ran a hand over my face with a frustrated sigh. Pursuing Lexi for anything more than a fling was out of the question. But denying my need for her left an empty ache in my gut.

Her dismissal last night had stung, but it only fueled my determination. I didn't agree with her reasons for pulling away, and I wasn't about to let them stop me.

This wasn't over. She could resist, but I knew how to break through her wall. The challenge now wasn't to have her in my arms again—it was to make her stay there.

Lexi finally eased herself into the chair beside Kneshel, setting down her mug and platter of fruits. Turning to Kneshel, Lexi playfully tickled Knöelle under her chin with a cooing sound. Her interaction with the baby was light and affectionate.

"Let me hold her, hon," Lexi offered, her arms already extended. "You should eat."

Kneshel looked grateful. "I won't say no to enjoying my food," she responded, carefully handing her daughter over.

As she cradled Knöelle, something unwelcome tugged in my chest at the sight. A flicker of longing for something I'd never considered before. Of Lexi, glowing with my child nestled in her arms.

I shook myself. Where had the thought come from?

Fatherhood had never been part of my plans. My work was my purpose, my pride and joy. And affairs with gorgeous, captivating women like Lexi were an enjoyable diversion, nothing more.

Try as I might to ignore the insidious thoughts, they crept in. A vision of Lexi, belly rounded, laughing as I kissed her stomach. Of a little girl with Lexi's sparkling eyes toddling into my arms. It unsettled me, this yearning for more than just the physical.

A baby? You're out of your mind. Lexi was a sweet fling at best, an intoxicating entanglement.

Those thoughts I determined were a product of too much ocean air. It made me soft. Made me imagine improbable things.

I forced my attention back to the idle breakfast chatter, grasping for my usual poise. But my eyes tracked Lexi as she stood and bounced Knöelle on her hip, murmuring to the baby. Knöelle pulled on the strap keeping Lexi's dress together and the neckline gaped open enough to give me a glimpse of the swells of her breasts.

I nearly groaned aloud. *Get it together, MJ.*

When Lexi returned to her seat with a now sleeping Knöelle, I leaned back and stretched. "You look a little tired this morning, Lexi. Did the noise last night keep you up?"

I kept my tone casual. I wanted to subtly remind her of how she came undone, crying out in ecstasy in my arms hours before.

Lexi's eyes darted to mine, widening. She then glanced down at the baby she held, a small intake of breath revealing her fluster.

"What noise?" Trina asked, puzzled.

I shrugged, grinning. "Moans and groans."

I watched in satisfaction as Lexi squirmed in her seat, color rising in her neck. When she crossed her legs, the slit in her dress fell open, exposing a long expanse of smooth, brown thigh. I nearly choked on my saliva, desire coursing through me.

"I slept very well, thank you," she replied smoothly. "This sea air is restful."

Kneshel jumped in. "Actually, I think what MJ heard was Lexi's TV. I heard it too."

Trina glanced at Lexi, brows furrowed. "There's no TV in Lexi's cabin."

I could no longer contain my smug grin as all eyes turned to Lexi. I awaited her response, hungry to see how she would wiggle her way out of this predicament.

"It was my laptop," she said at last. "I was streaming *Sundance Beach*, and I guess the speakers were too loud." She gave an embarrassed little laugh.

I had to hand it to her. She played it off beautifully. But the delightful blush staining her chest gave her away, revealing the truth only we knew. I had never enjoyed flustering someone so much. This vacation might prove more entertaining than I imagined.

"I love that show!" Amy, who was stacking pancakes on her plate said. "Gabby and Aaron are my favorite characters! They're endgame for sure!"

Joy shook her head. "I love Aaron and Mia as a couple. But what do you think Diego's mother is hiding?"

For the next several moments, the other women debated furiously, their voices rising in pitch, each arguing for their favorite pairing or plot twist. I kept my gaze on Lexi as she nodded and laughed along with the conversation, mesmerized by the play of emotions on her face.

"You know," Lexi mused, her voice tinged with a thoughtfulness. "Sometimes it's not about whether two people are meant to be, but whether they're ready for each other. Gabby and Aaron... they still have so much to learn about themselves."

She was an adept actress, able to participate in their conversation while concealing my effect on her. I felt a pang of longing to be alone with her again, to share in that private world where we could be entirely open with each other.

I moved closer to her while everyone else was distracted and asked, "Last night's plot was beyond your satisfaction?" Anyone else would assume I was speaking of the actual television show, but she knew exactly what I meant.

To my surprise, Lexi merely shrugged as she speared a bit of papaya with her fork and stuck it in her mouth. "It was okay. Nothing to write home about."

I blinked, wrongfooted. Only okay? I racked my brain, certain our passionate encounter had left her crying my name in ecstasy.

Lexi gave me a coy smile. "Well, the grip on me was certainly strong and... enthusiastic," she paused. "But honestly, the plot was a bit uninspired. And the climax came much too quickly."

Studying her face, I tried to discern if she was serious. Around us, the others continued chattering, oblivious to our coded discussion.

"I was expecting more creativity, more nuance," she continued airily. "It could have benefitted from stronger... development."

I shifted in my seat, intrigued. But before I could say any more to Lexi, I felt a tugging on my sleeves.

It was my sister's adopted daughter, Aisha. Her skin was a warm golden brown, smooth and unblemished, like milky tea. A mop of loose black curls cascaded down her back with a few strands escaping the purple hair clip attempting to constrain them.

"Uncle MJ, can you hold Izzy for me while I eat?" She held out a floppy baby doll swaddled in many layers of clothes and blankets. If she had been a real baby, she would have gotten heatstroke.

I took the doll carefully, making a big show of cradling her as if she was real. Not that I'd had much experience in handling babies, but I'd seen both Kneshel and Lexi hold earlier.

Aisha seemed satisfied and began eating her breakfast with gusto. I watched her for a few more moments, shoveling pancakes and vegan bacon into her mouth. Although both of my sisters stuck to their childhood vegan diet, I'd long ago succumbed to the siren call of meat and poultry.

When I turned my attention back to Lexi, I found a fond smile playing at the corners of her mouth. Before I could ask Lexi for redemption, Trina called for our attention.

"The animators for the ceramics will arrive within the hour. I've set up everything in the lounge."

"Bestie, don't you mean your staff had everything prepared?" Marlowe chimed in. Hazel and Marlowe clinked their glasses as they giggled.

Joy leaned over to Marlowe, eyes dancing. "Leave it to you to keep it real, girl."

I was almost surprised when Lexi spoke up and added, "The staff may do all the heavy lifting. But we still appreciate you organizing the fun, Trina."

Trina laughed, waving her hand dismissively at the other women, and turned to Lexi. "Thank you for recognizing my hard work, girl!" Her expression turned impish. "I'm looking for a new sister and best friend. You're welcome to both positions."

Lexi grinned. "Good to know." She shot a sly look at Marlowe.

Trina placed a hand over her heart. "I promise glam trips, endless spa days, and the cutest godchildren you can handle!"

"Arslan is my godson forever," Marlowe said breezily. "You're stuck with my fabulous self, Trina."

The mood was light and lively, and I felt content to be amongst it. I caught Lexi's eye with a meaningful look. There were still unresolved matters between us, but for now, I was happy to enjoy the leisurely morning unfolding.

After the laughter died down, Trina continued, listing the expectations for the activity. There was a pleased murmur among the women.

"It sounds fun," Joy said enthusiastically.

Trina turned to me and stated, "You're participating."

I cringed. I didn't have a single artistic bone in my body.

"Do you have any memories of me even drawing as a kid? I'm awful at this stuff."

"I don't," Trina said. "But I want you to try it!"

I grabbed my sister's hand pleadingly. "A raincheck? Please?"

She shook her head. I sighed and resigned myself to spending my day smeared in paint and coughing out clay dust.

I noticed Lexi's small smile at my discomfort and in the sweetest tones, she asked to be excused from the activity because of jetlag. She also brought up the flight to Italy was her first ever. Naturally, this afforded her Trina's sympathy, understanding and encouragement for rest.

Soon enough, the other women and kids filed out, all heading off to prepare for their craft class, leaving Lexi alone with me. Lexi picked up her plate, carrying it to the sideboard rather than allow a steward to remove it for her.

I moved swiftly, positioning myself between her and the wall, cutting off her escape. When she turned, she was face-to-face with my chest, her eyes widening in surprise.

I didn't move, didn't give her space to retreat. I wanted her to feel my presence, to know I wasn't stepping back.

"You require a more complex storyline?"

"Well, I..." She faltered, tongue-tied suddenly.

"I don't mind delivering another performance worthy of Lexis Voss' five-star praise..." I said, running my fingers over her loose braids, waiting for her to blush, to fluster.

But she smiled and said, "I'm sure the ceramics class will be more than enough excitement for you today."

I stepped closer. Close enough to notice the top of her bikini being held together by two connected silver rings, and the halter strap behind her neck was only single-knotted with the kind of bow you put on top of a present. I could undo it with a simple tug.

"Marcus..." she began, licking her lips. "Someone could walk in and get the wrong idea if they see us standing so close."

I paused, eyebrows raising at the sound of my full name on her lips. It stirred a surprising ache in my chest, reminding me of my mother's gentle chiding when I was a boy up to mischief.

"Marcus?" I repeated. "I can't recall the last time someone used my actual name." I reached out, brushing my knuckles lightly along her cheek. "But I find I don't mind it from your lips.

"Your ceramics class..."

"Can wait." I groaned, dropping my head atop hers in exaggerated dismay. "I was hoping you'd help me sneak away from that torture."

Lexi laughed, the sound warming me like sunlight while nudging me lightly in the chest. "Oh no, I think getting in touch with your creative side could be good for you."

"Maybe you're right..." I let a slow grin spread across my face. "This ceramic class could allow me the opportunity to flex my creative talents."

"I hope you find your muse today. Who knows where it may lead?"

"To you, of course," I said, stepping closer. My voice dropped lower, teasing. "I can't stop thinking about the way you moaned my name last night. And if you want more... complexity, I'm ready to give it to you. Whenever you're ready."

Her eyes flickered with something between amusement and desire, but I didn't blink. I wouldn't give up until she was beneath me, lost in the same fervor from Valentine's Day.

With effort, I stepped back, though my eyes lingered on her a moment longer. As much as I wanted to pull her into my arms, she had a point.

"You're right," I conceded. "I don't want to make you the subject of gossip among my family or to make you feel uncomfortable on this yacht."

Lexi gave me a tremulous smile. "Thank you for understanding."

She moved to step around me, but I caught her arm. I lifted her hand to my lips, pressing a lingering kiss to her wrist.

"This isn't over, Lexi," I whispered against her skin, my gaze locking onto hers.

She pulled her hand back, but I could see the way her breath quickened, the way her pulse raced under my fingers. I let her go for now. But I wasn't done. Not until she was mine again.

Lexi

I nsomnia was a curse, and I was willing to go stand naked at a crossroads and chant whatever incantations were necessary to lift it. The only time I'd gotten a decent sleep in recent years was Valentine's night. Sleep had eluded me for many nights since then restful slumber and it felt like a distant memory now.

My sleep troubles began after my parents' tragic and untimely deaths fourteen years ago. That horrific night haunted me, playing over and over in my mind whenever I lie in bed. I remembered the last time I'd seen my parents alive. I could see the scene clearly.

They'd been bickering about my nineteen-year-old sister Tiffany's relationship with Allan. My father didn't like the young man, while my mom came to their defense.

"You were twenty when I met you at nineteen. My parents couldn't convince me our love wasn't real. Give them a chance," my mom reminded him.

In response, my father harrumphed dismissively.

I never forgot the sound because it was the last thing I heard from my dad. The next time I saw them was in their caskets.

Vivid images of them lying in those timber boxes always invaded my attempts at sleep. I'd seen countless grief counselors and tried several remedies. Nothing worked better than a long stroll before bed... or an orgasm.

I got up, pulled an oversized t-shirt over my head, and slipped on a pair of sandals. When I opened the door of my cabin, I almost expected to find Marcus hovering near my door and was disappointed he wasn't.

Since Kneshel had proven to be as sharp-eared as a fruit bat, I tiptoed past her door, reluctant to get into any conversation about why I was wandering around the ship at night.

Keeping to the center of the hallways and nodding at Trina's security detail, I made my way to the upper deck where my favorite pool was. To my mild disappointment, someone was already there.

The last thing I wanted was company. But then the symmetry of the dark, elegant shape caught my eye, and I knew it could only be one person.

Marcus.

I halted in the shadows, my breath catching at the sight before me. Marcus moved through the glowing blue water with powerful strokes, utterly oblivious to my presence.

I should slip away before he noticed me. This encounter could only lead to temptation and trouble, but I remained rooted in place, helpless to tear my eyes from him.

Lean muscles flexed in his arms as he flipped and pushed off the wall in a smooth tumble turn. My pulse quickened watching him.

How many nights had I lain awake remembering the feel of those muscular arms around me?

"You can join me, you know."

Marcus' voice made me start. He treaded water, eyes glinting knowingly at my hesitation.

Every instinct told me to turn and flee, to retreat to my cabin, but something about the way Marcus moved through the water, so sure of himself, held me in place. My mind raced, reminding me of all the reasons I should walk away, but I remained rooted to the spot.

"Swimming's good for insomnia." His tone held a hint of teasing and challenge. "Google it. It's a thing."

I clutched the hem of the t-shirt, tempted to cast it off and plunge into the water. I imagined the exhilaration of the turquoise water enveloping my heated skin.

"I don't have a swimsuit," I pointed out.

Marcus shrugged, muscles rippling as he glided to the pool's edge and looped his arms over the side. "Hey, if you want to skinny dip, no judgment here."

I took a deep breath, trying to shake off the enticing images Marcus's words had conjured. Skinny dipping with him was out of the question, but the allure of the cool water proved too tempting to resist.

Slowly, I stepped out of the shadows and made my way to the edge of the pool. I sat down, letting my legs dangle in the water.

The water felt refreshing against my skin, and I let out a contented sigh.

Marcus swam closer, his eyes never leaving mine. He propped his arms on the edge of the pool, mere inches from where I sat.

Droplets of water glistened on his bronze skin, and I resisted the urge to reach out and trace the paths they made down his sculpted chest. Instinctively, I shifted away, just a fraction, trying to maintain some semblance of distance.

"How was your ceramics class?"

He grimaced. "Oh, you know, broke a few things and started over three times."

"The usual, then," I said this with a smile, having zero regrets about missing the activity.

While I appreciated Trina's efforts to keep us entertained, I knew my strengths lay in stitching up wounds and caring for patients. I thought of my boss, Dr. Forrest Parsons, who always joked I was the Van Gogh of the butterfly suture. I smiled at the memory, remembering the satisfaction I felt when I could help others, even in the smallest ways.

Marcus grinned.

The ensuing silence between us was surprisingly comfortable. My feet didn't twitch with the desire to run away.

Marcus sniffed deeply, looking at the glittering, inky black sky overhead. "It's been ages since I took a vacation like this," he commented.

"Really? I'd have thought living in Asia offered endless opportunities to explore."

He gave a slight shake of his head, water droplets flying from his damp curls. "Work keeps me busy most days. I'm usually holed up in my office reviewing case files or prepping for court."

My mind wandered back to our night in Montrose. In the aftermath of our second round of lovemaking, Marcus had confessed his longing for a change of pace and a desire to spend more time with his father.

Despite knowing Marcus harbored no genuine feelings for me, I had silently wished for him to secure the position at the university. I felt an inexplicable urge to keep him close, indulging in fantasies of catching glimpses of him around town.

"All work and no play makes Marcus a dull boy," I quipped, and regretted saying it almost immediately. "I'm sorry... I didn't mean that."

"You're right. I could use more balance in my life." He moved closer to me. "Maybe you could help me with my balancing act," he said, voice low and suggestive.

"I'm not sure I'm the right person for that," I said, offering him a small smile. "My life is pretty simple. Work, walking my dogs, and the occasional TV binge. Nothing too adventurous."

I kept my tone light, but I felt the weight of the truth in my words. I wasn't someone who sought out excitement, and I wasn't sure I was ready for the kind of intensity Marcus brought into my life.

Marcus tilted his head, gaze turning thoughtful as he studied my face. His eyes dropped to my lips before meeting my eyes again.

"I have a feeling you could show me all kinds of new adventures."

I took a small step back, though my body yearned to move closer. "Careful, I might drag you along on neighborhood watch meetings and grocery runs if you're not specific," I joked.

Marcus grinned, playing along. "I was thinking more along the lines of moonlit swims, stargazing on the deck..." His voice dipped lower... "and perhaps some late-night dancing in my cabin," he finished, his eyes twinkling with playful mischief.

His gaze locked with mine, forming an electric connection. My heart pounded relentlessly against my ribcage. I couldn't help but glance at his lips before meeting his eyes once more.

Swallowing hard, I struggled to compose myself, the intensity of the moment threatening to overwhelm me. "You can't dance," I reminded him.

"You're right. I have all the grace of a drunken giraffe on the dance floor."

I giggled at the unexpected image, the sound bubbling up before I could stop it. Marcus's smile widened, his eyes crinkling at the corners.

"How many siblings do you have?" he asked unexpectedly.

"It's just my sister, Tiffany, and me. She's eight years older." I pictured Tiffany's kind eyes and uninhibited laughter. "Most of my free time outside of work is spent with my sister, her kids, and my fur babies."

"Your sister must appreciate you," he said somberly. "Family is everything."

"It's just the two of us now. Our parents died when I was eleven years old."

They had been killed while crossing the street to get to a restaurant. The person behind the wheel was a teenager who had been texting while driving and missed the stop.

As I spoke, my hand came up unconsciously to my forearm, absently stroking the tattoos of their names. My mother had died on the scene, and my father passed less than two hours later at the hospital.

"My mom's best friend, Aunt Sheryl, took us both in after the deaths and saw to all our immediate needs. I will forever cherish those two years we lived with her while Tiffany sorted out my guardianship and her own career path."

My mind drifted to Ben, a knot forming in my stomach. I should tell Marcus about Ben and our engagement. It wasn't fair to keep him in the dark, even if what Ben and I had wasn't real.

But as I looked at Marcus, I hesitated. Did he really need to know? This... whatever this was between us, wasn't meant to last.

Still, the thought of deceiving him, even by omission, didn't sit well with me.

By now, he was seated at the pool's edge next to me and regarding me solemnly. "I'm glad you had people to care for you." His thumb brushed over my knuckles. "But I wish you'd never gone through such a loss."

"Me too." I wiped at my eyes, feeling suddenly self-conscious.

He wrapped his arms around me and pulled me against him. I was rigid at first, surprised by the intimacy of the moment. But then I allowed myself to relax into his embrace.

My body fit snugly against his, the cool dampness of his skin seeping through my clothes. His chin rested atop my head as we sat there in a silent communion beneath the star-studded sky.

If I was thinking straight, I'd have wriggled out of his grasp, but instead my treacherous body leaned in further. His bare, muscular chest felt like a homecoming.

"You've endured a lot. I admire your strength."

Tilting my face up to meet his, a flicker of something raw and unguarded played in his eyes before he dipped his head to capture my lips. The kiss was slow and unhurried. His lips moved against mine with languid intensity and it slowly unraveling me.

I sank into him, my arms looping around his neck as our bodies drew flush against each other. He tasted like chlorine and summer. His tongue explored my mouth, firm and insistent, yet incredibly gentle. It was a sweet exploration.

We finally broke the kiss, but didn't pull apart. His eyes gleamed down at me, radiating warmth.

I hesitated for a moment, feeling the weight of the intimacy we'd just shared. Part of me wanted to slip back into the safety of my cabin, to create some distance before I let this go any further.

But the pull of Marcus was undeniable, and against my better judgment, I allowed myself to smile. "I think I'm ready for that swim," I said, though a small voice in the back of my mind warned me to be careful.

Amid the chaos of breakfast—children playing, adults chatting—Marcus' steady gaze sought mine. The connection between us was palpable, and I was acutely aware of the electrifying effect his stare had on me.

My mind drifted back to the previous night when he had gathered me in his arms and I had wrapped my legs around his waist. Our mouths had met in a series of heated, open-mouthed kisses as he walked us into the water while I was still clothed.

We had played and teased like giddy kids, splashing and dunking each other, our laughter echoing off the darkened deck. When our play wound down, we had treaded water and talked in hushed voices about everything and nothing. The intimacy of our whispered conversation under the stars made my heart swell even though I knew this thing between us was temporary.

By the time I returned to my cabin, I'd gone over every possible reason why this thing with Marcus was a bad idea. It was temporary, it was reckless, and I knew I could get hurt.

But something about him made it hard to think rationally, and for the second time in my life, I wanted to let go. I wanted to throw caution to the wind, even if my heart warned me against it.

"This must be the most uneventful vacation you've ever been on, Lexi," Marlowe said sympathetically, right after Trina announced that she'd organized a picnic at a local park. "No partying, no nightlife. Just a bunch of kids and their moms, talking about diaper rash, nipple creams, and dinosaur-shaped chicken tenders."

The look Hazel and Joy gave me as they nodded in agreement was almost pitying.

I quickly assured them, "I'm not bored at all."

How could I be, when Marcus Davis Junior looked at me like I was the only star in his universe?? Kissed me as if he was parched and I was the only source of water in a scorching desert?

"I'm perfectly happy to be here," I assured them, offering a warm smile. "I'm having a great time, really."

Even as I spoke, I made a mental note to check in with Kneshel later. She'd looked tired this morning, and I wanted to make sure she was okay. It was easy to get caught up in my own thoughts, but I didn't want to lose sight of the people around me.

"I've been reading about Capri's must-see sights," I continued. "I plan to spend today walking around the piazza."

Before Marcus and I parted last night, we had agreed the best way to be alone was to leave the yacht separately and meet up in town. The secrecy only added to the thrill.

"All on your own?" Marcus Sr. frowned as he looked across the table at me. "A single woman? In a foreign country?" He looked as though the idea scandalized his sensibilities. "Tell me dear, have you been off the boat alone before?"

"No, but I—"

"Junior! Are you hearing this?" The senior Marcus turned to his son. "We can't let this young lady wander around this town alone. There are people out there who will pounce on her like a wolf on a lamb. What are you doing today?"

Marcus's surprise at being summarily addressed was almost comical. He opened his mouth to respond, but his dad never gave him the chance.

"Never mind that. Today, you're to escort this young lady around town." He waved his hand with the authority only parents wield, not seeming to care that his son was a grown man. "Do you hear me, son?"

Marcus Jr. was struggling not to laugh. "Yes, Dad. I hear you."

"That sounds like a wonderful plan." Trina enthused. "Lexi will get to do something more fun than picnicking with toddlers, and she'll be safe with MJ."

Marcus and I exchanged amused glances. Last night, we'd spent plenty of time devising cover stories to sneak away together, and now, the perfect opportunity had fallen right into our laps.

Grinning, Marcus stood from the table, not bothering to hide his amusement. He walked over to my side and, in an exaggerated gesture, bowed deeply like a Victorian gentleman inviting a duchess to dance.

"Lady Lexi," he declared, loud enough for everyone to hear, "would you do me the honor of allowing me to escort you on your promenade?"

I caught on immediately and played along. Offering him my hand, which he kissed theatrically, I replied in my best Brontë-inspired voice, "Your kindness is most... unexpected, sir. It would be improper of me to refuse such a chivalrous offer."

Around us, the other women laughed.

MJ

I glanced down at Lexi, unable to resist the sight of her pink tongue whipping out to swirl around the tip of the cone. The sight of it almost made me drop my vanilla gelato.

She eyed my gelato. "Vanilla is the most boring flavor in the world."

"Boring, you say?" I questioned, letting the cool of the vanilla gelato paint my tongue. "I prefer to think of it as a classic."

Lexi rolled her eyes, but her smile never faltered. She darted forward suddenly, her pink tongue reaching out to swipe at my vanilla cone. Surprised, I could only watch as she pulled away with a satisfied grin.

"Vanilla isn't so bad, is it?" I shot back.

She stuck out her tongue, revealing a white smear of vanilla. Without hesitation, I leaned down, capturing her tongue in my mouth.

She squealed in surprise before her free hand crept up to grip my shoulder, holding on to me as we explored each other's tastes. The cool hint of vanilla was still there, now intermingling with the tart flavor of her raspberry sorbet.

Our world condensed down to the taste of our sweet treats and each other, the warmth of the sun overhead, and the slight breeze making Lexi's dress dance.

"Well, it does taste better when it's on your tongue," Lexi said when we finally broke apart.

I chuckled and took a moment to catch my breath, the taste of her still lingering in my mouth. "I couldn't agree more."

We fell into a comfortable silence as we continued walking side by side, eating our cold treats. We strolled past colorful market stalls and fishermen tending to their nets, the warm breeze carrying the scent of salt and fresh seafood.

"I can't believe we got away so easily," Lexi said when we approached the piazza.

"Believe it," I answered, my smirk unfaltering. "Thanks to my noble father, who would never allow a lady to be at risk."

I wondered if my dad had been more deliberate in his insistence than anyone suspected. Was he aware of my attraction to Lexi?

We explored in earnest, slipping into small shops half-hidden down twisting cobbled side streets. Lexi stood before each plate-glass window, staring in like a kid outside a candy shop, and once she saw something she liked, she dragged me in by the wrist inside.

"Tiffany would love these," she mused, her fingers lightly tracing over the detailed beadwork on a striking pair of leather sandals.

"Are you planning to buy out the entire island?" I asked teasingly, my gaze softening as I watched her. The way her eyes sparkled every time we discovered something new was truly a sight to behold.

Ignoring my remark, Lexi slipped off her sneakers and tried on the sandals. As she did, I noticed an old man sitting in the corner, his gnarled hands moving deftly as he meticulously crafted yet another pair of sandals.

"My sister and I are the same shoe size and these fit," Lexi announced, a triumphant grin spreading across her face.

With the new sandals snug in her tote, we left the shop. Lexi paused to absorb the vibrant street life that unfolded with every step.

I watched her, appreciating the way her eyes drank in the details, a soft smile playing on her lips. I was having the best day, walking next to her, holding her hands, kissing her spontaneously.

"Ooh."

Lexi froze, staring down at a pair of silver filigree earrings, loops of metal embracing a small freshwater pearl. We were in a jewelry store.

"That is...." She seemed to be struggling to find the words to express her feelings. "It's..." She inhaled and shook her head.

"It's yours," I said firmly, calling the sales agent over.

"What?" she squeaked in protest. "No! Did you see the price tag on that thing?"

I gave her an amused look. "I have. Clearly, they value it as highly as you do."

The cost of some of my dinners at restaurants exceeded the price of the earrings. I wanted to spoil her, give her everything she desired. This was a completely new experience for me, unlike anything I had felt for anyone else.

Lexi began to protest once more, but I silenced her by placing my mouth over hers and sticking my tongue inside. Lexi's surprise melted into surrender. She kissed me back enthusiastically.

When we pulled apart, breathing heavily, I could see the flush on Lexi's cheeks. Her eyes darkened with desire. I winked at her before turning to the middle-aged sales agent who had been watching our exchange amusedly.

The man didn't speak English. Mastercard, however, was an international language.

Less than two minutes later, I removed the summery baubles dangling from her earlobes and replaced them with the fine silver earrings. They looked incongruous when contrasted with the modernity of her facial piercings, but the glow of delight on her face made it all worthwhile.

The sun was high up in the sky when we left the jewelry store. The heat felt almost cloying as we made our way through the streets hand-in-hand.

"Hungry?" I asked, breaking the comfortable silence between us.

"Hmm," Lexi nodded, her brows knitting together as she contemplated. "I could kill for some calamari and pasta."

We found a small handmade pasta restaurant tucked away in a corner, owned by an old couple whose smiles were as warm as the ovens they used to prepare their food. The tantalizing smell of pesto and tomato sauce filled the air, making me suddenly aware of my own hunger.

Lexi ordered calamari for an appetizer and ricotta and spinach ravioli with butter and sage, which she insisted was adventurous, while I went for pomodoro.

When the food arrived, I twirled long strips of linguini around my fork and held it out to her. She'd called my lunch order boring, and I wanted to prove a point.

"Taste this," I commanded. "You'll see how perfect simplicity can be."

She parted her pink lips and chewed, closing her eyes. Then she licked her lips and gave a soft sigh. My dick grew rock hard.

"Okay... okay, pomodoro isn't boring," she admitted, opening her eyes. The soft afternoon light filtered through the restaurant's small windows, providing her brown skin with an ethereal glow.

"I knew you'd see the light," I said. Lexi playfully rolled her eyes, taking a bite out of her own ravioli.

The next day, we relied on our ingenuity to meet up in town. Lexi was able to excuse herself from the parent and child activity Trina planned. As for me, I mollified my sisters by spending the morning with them, leaving me free to slip away by early afternoon.

We left the yacht separately and met at the café we'd stumbled on the day before. It was right next to the harbor. We sat there for a while over coffee, allowing our psyches to get used to the idea of being alone together before hiking Monte Solaro.

As we climbed our way up the mountain, a sense of tranquility wrapped around me. The scent of exotic flowers, carried on the gentle Mediterranean breeze, filled my nostrils while the distant sound of waves crashing against the rocky coastline provided a soothing soundtrack for our journey.

Lexi, with her camera in hand, kept wandering off the designated trail to take photographs of the picturesque scenery. I took this opportunity to appreciate her. I loved the way she carried herself, and how easy it was to speak to her.

"Look at the view," Lexi gestured towards the edge of a cliff, where the sapphire blue sea met the azure sky at the horizon.

"There's nothing in this world that comes close to matching that."

I looked at her then, her face radiant in the sunshine. "I can think of one thing."

Startled by my sudden seriousness, Lexi turned around to look at me.

"What?" she asked after a moment of silence.

"You," I said before pulling her into a passionate kiss.

The world fell away as we stood together on the cliff's edge, the heat of our bodies contrasting with the cool ocean breeze. I considered dragging her into a nearby flowering bush and having my way with her.

The sound of footsteps brought an end to those thoughts. I reluctantly pulled back, breathless and aroused.

"Come on," I whispered, interlacing our fingers together. "Let's see what else this mountain has to offer."

We continued our journey up Monte Solaro in pleasant chatter, teasing and occasionally slipping into more serious topics as we got to know each other better.

"I know how much you were looking forward to it," she said, hugging me after I'd told her about not getting the position at Montrose University. I held her tight, breathing in the hibiscus scent of her hair. "I'm sorry."

"It's alright," I replied with a smile, my gaze focused on the trail ahead, before pulling away. "Everything happens for a reason, as they say."

Lexi squeezed my hand in silent understanding. Silence enveloped us as we continued our walk, our footfalls the only sound.

Over the next several days, the pattern continued, each day a new adventure, each night in bed alone, a new exploration of unexpected emotions. We visited the local markets, experienced the traditional cuisine, and even attended a local festival celebrating the island's heritage. We danced in the streets with locals and tourists alike, losing ourselves in the music's rhythm and the liveliness of the celebration.

One day, I hired a small boat to go sailing around the island. Lexi's braids moved freely in the wind as she laughed, her joy echoing off the water. I was content watching her, my heart filling with happiness every time she smiled.

"Have you ever done anything like this before?" she asked me, her eyes never leaving mine.

I shook my head. "I've sailed before, but never with companions as intriguing as you." Lexi blushed at my words, but her smile remained wide.

The following evening, we sank into comfortable chairs at a cliff side bar, where we ordered drinks and tapas. I watched, mesmerized, as Lexi sipped her drink, her eyes closed in pleasure.

"I love limoncello! I have to take some home with me!"

As we indulged in our food, we let the atmosphere of the island slip into our conversation. The jovial laughter of locals nearby, the lapping waves against the rocks below the cliff, and the occasional burst of fireworks from some celebration at a distance. Soaking in this exquisite tranquility, I couldn't help but wonder if this was what bliss felt like.

There was laughter at the entrance of the bar, and when I looked up, I spotted an unexpected and unwelcome sight.

"Quickly," I whispered, grabbing her hand and pulling her up from her chair.

Lexi looked startled, her eyes wide and questioning. "What's wrong?"

"No time," I said, tossing a few Euro notes on the table.

Taking her hand, we slipped into a narrow side alley, away from the bar and the patrons. As we made our way down the dimly lit passageway, Lexi finally wrenched her hand away.

"Marcus! Stop!" she demanded, panting slightly from our quick pace. "Tell me what's going on."

I turned around to face her, took a quick glance over her head to ensure we hadn't been followed. The coast was clear for now. I took both of her hands in mine, attempting to calm the panic in her eyes.

"My sisters are here. Along with the others."

Understanding dawned on Lexi's face. "Do you think they saw us?"

"I don't think so," I admitted, my brows furrowing in thought. "But I didn't want to risk it. I know you want to keep this thing between us under wraps."

"Thank you," she said, her gaze dropping to our entwined hands. "This all seems silly."

"Silly?" I echoed, a slight frown creasing my forehead.

I tried not to let my disappointment seep into my voice, but the word stung. Silly was buying too many souvenirs or placing a saucer of milk outside for the stray cats at their hotel.

"No, not like that," Lexi corrected quickly, lifting her gaze to meet mine. There was an apology in her eyes. "I mean sneaking around like this... It's exhilarating, but also..."

"Ridiculous?" I suggested, chuckling lightly. She joined me, and for a moment, we were simply two people laughing together in a dimly lit alleyway in Capri.

"If keeping things between us private is important to you, it's important to me." I moved a braid from her face and tucked it behind her ear, tracing my fingers down to her cheek.

Lexi's hands traveled to my head and gently pulled me lower, placing a soft kiss on my lips. "I appreciate your indulgence, Marcus," she whispered against my lips.

Hidden away in the shadows of an Italian alleyway, I felt myself falling for her. Her vulnerability, her sweetness, her fiery spirit...

All of it was intoxicating. I wanted more. More of her smiles, more of her laughter, more of her soft touches and gentle kisses.

I led us through the labyrinthine streets of the town, away from the bar where my sisters and their friends had appeared. We slowly made our way back to *Inescapable* under the starlit sky.

"Fancy visiting Villa Jovis tomorrow?" I asked, breaking the comfortable silence between us. "The Emperor who once lived there allegedly threw his enemies into the sea."

Lexi hesitated at first, but seemed to warm up to the idea rather quickly. "I would love to." She nodded with a smile playing on her lips. "I could use some more pictures."

I smiled, my voice low and deliberate. "And I could use more time with you."

MJ

The next morning dawned with a gentle breeze that carried the promise of adventure. I rose with the first light, the anticipation of the day ahead fueling my steps. It was a couple of hours later, as the town began to stir, that Lexi, with the soft glow of the morning sun on her face, made her way to our café.

We made the winding drive up the mountainside, following the switchbacks as we ascended towards the ancient villa. The sea breeze brought with it the sweet scent of the island's citrus groves and wildflowers. Now and then, Lexi would point out a stunning vista or a unique bird that had darted past.

When we reached our destination, we started the hike up to Villa Jovis, chatting animatedly and laughing at each other's jokes. As we walked through the lush gardens of the villa, Lexi took her time, snapping pictures of the stunning panoramas that spread out before us, framing Capri's rugged beauty.

The ruins of the villa were a quiet place. The chirping of birds and rustling of windswept trees were the only sounds as we wandered through what was left of Tiberius's grand palace. We took our time exploring each crumbling room and terrace.

Grabbing Lexi's hand, I pulled her into an empty room. We fell upon each other with an intensity born of high adrenaline from our walk and our lingering hunger for each other that had been brewing over the past few days.

The kiss intensified. We grew bolder as we touched, felt, and explored each other. Her body was warm from the sun, pliant, and smelled of honey, grass, and sweat. It excited me more than I thought possible.

Lexi kissed a trail down my body until she was kneeling before me, eager hands reaching for the front of my pants. I didn't think to protest, not caring we were in a public place with tourists milling about.

I lost all thoughts when her hands freed my dick and began stroking and pumping me with her hands before taking me into her mouth. It was surprisingly cool, the icy feeling lingering from the drink she'd just had. Also, the hint of lemons made me tingle.

She sucked and flicked her tongue against my tip and swirled it around my length repeatedly while pumping me with her hands. I had to bite down on a groan, my hands clenching her braids tightly. I looked down at her, my body shuddering under the waves of pleasure coursing through me.

And then there was a sharp peal of laughter, a sound that echoed from wall to wall. Someone was coming. "Lexi... stop," I breathed out, my voice shaky. She glanced up at me, her eyes twinkling with mischief and desire.

I wanted to push her away, but the wildness in her eyes stopped me and instead, I pumped harder and deeper down her throat even while footsteps came nearer. On the brink of ecstasy now, I tried pulling away, not wanting to finish in her mouth, but she only sucked me faster, her hands moving in sync with her mouth.

I let out a low guttural groan, surrendering to the moment, and exploded down her willing throat. I watched in amazement as she swallowed every drop of my cum before freeing me from her warm mouth and tucking me back into my shorts.

Pulling her up towards me, I kissed her passionately, tasting myself on her tongue. My hands gripped her ass as I pressed her body against the ancient stone wall of the room, hungry again for her touch, her taste.

A small group of people passed by along an adjacent corridor, and none turned our way. "Payback's a Lexi, huh?" she teased with a grin after we broke the kiss.

I chuckled, resting my chin atop her head. "I guess so," I said, my heart pounding wildly in my chest as I slowly started gaining control of myself. I stared down at her for a second, disbelief and amusement swimming in my eyes. "Did you plan this?"

Lexi shrugged, keeping her gaze locked with mine. "It was a spur-of-the-moment decision. I saw an opportunity, and I took it."

"Well, it's your turn," I said and before she could say anymore, I claimed her lips once again, this time with fervor and a promise of more.

Running my hands up her thighs, I hiked up the light summer skirt she wore. She gasped into my mouth, her hands flying up to my shoulders for support.

I smiled against her lips, feeling a rush of power and satisfaction as she moaned when my hands reached the lacy edge of her underwear and I could feel how ready she was, how wet she was for me. I cupped her pussy, my fingers trailing over the sensitive folds, soaking in the feel of her.

Lexi's breath hitched in response, her eyes closing as a whimper escaped her lips. A wave of raw desire coursed through me as I slid my fingers under the lace, carefully exploring the hot wetness beneath it.

Breathing in the scent of her skin, I kissed the soft curve of her neck, making her shiver in my arms. When I slipped a finger inside her, her gasp of pleasure was music to my ears.

As I began to move in rhythm with her body, I felt her curve against me, her walls clenching around my fingers. The quiet moans escaped her lips were swallowed by my opened mouth kiss.

I added another finger, stretching and filling her as I continued to move rhythmically against her. She gasped out my name, her hands clutching at my back. With a sudden jerky movement, she rocked against my hand and let out a soft cry.

Her thighs clenching around my thrusting hand signaled she was teetering on the edge of release. I increased my pace, wanting nothing more than to see her crumple with pleasure under my touch.

Suddenly, her body stiffened as she let out a stifled whimper. Her eyes were locked onto mine as she rode out the wave of pleasure washing over her. I felt her body quake under me, and it filled me with a sense of pride and accomplishment.

Once she'd caught her breath, I eased my fingers out of her and lifted the hand to my lips, tasting the sweetness of her release. She watched me through heavy-lidded eyes, a flush spreading across her face.

Suddenly, the sound of approaching voices snapped us back to reality. We quickly stepped apart, trying to fix our disheveled appearances. A group of tourists walked past us, chattering excitedly about Roman mosaics and Tiberius's reign.

Once they were out of earshot, Lexi burst into laughter. "That was...exhilarating," she finished, her eyes still dancing with wicked amusement.

"To say the least," I agreed, pulling her back into my arms.

The rest of the day passed in a blur of laughter and stolen kisses, every quiet corner an opportunity for another private moment. As the sun began to set, we made our way back down towards the yacht.

During dinner, I couldn't take my eyes off Lexi. She wore a pink maxi dress with a slit up to her hip bone, revealing tantalizing glimpses of her bare legs.

My fingers itched to touch her, to pull her closer until our bodies were pressed together. Occasionally, she'd catch me staring and give me a sly smile.

"MJ," Trina started. "Were you at a cliff side bar in town recently?"

I exchanged a quick glance with Lexi before turning back to my sister. "Why do you ask?"

"Joy thought she might have seen you," Trina said, swirling the wine in her glass. "With a woman. But by the time she pointed the man out to me, he was no longer there."

"Must've been someone else," I said smoothly, keeping my tone even.

Trina seemed to accept this explanation, dropping her line of questioning and turning to speak to Kneshel.

Later that night, after dinner, when everyone started to retire for the night, I touched Lexi's hand as she walked by me. "Come to my cabin tonight," I whispered quietly as she continued.

Hours later, I was lying on my bed with my hands behind my head when I heard a muted sound outside my door. The door pushed open and Lexi entered, closing and locking it behind her. She still wore the dress from earlier.

"You asked me to come," she stated. She looked slightly unsure, eyes darting over my naked body.

I tried to hide my excitement at having her there and patted my lap in response. "C'mere."

Lexi lingered over to me, removing her dress as she walked. Under the dress, she wore only a delicate lace bra and for a moment I forgot to breathe.

As she climbed onto the bed and straddled my lap, I positioned her core over my shaft without entering her. I groaned at the feel of her warmth and wetness.

"You're beautiful," I murmured and began trailing kisses over her face and neck.

It delighted me to know since putting those earrings on her earlobes, she hadn't taken them off. I wished I'd bought her more jewelry. Imagined what she'd look like with pearls around her neck, her wrists, stomach and ankles.

It would be my mark on her.

Her hands came up to cup my face as she leaned in, kissing me passionately. I could taste the lingering sweetness of the wine we had shared over dinner. Her hips instinctively ground against my erection while we kissed. My need for her was as palpable as hers was for me.

My hands slid down her body, outlining each curve, each dip and ridge, until they rested on her hips. She moaned as my hands cupped her backside, propelling her body in motion so her clit rubbed against my length. With deft fingers, I undid the clasps of her bra, letting the fabric fall away to reveal the exquisite artistry of her breasts.

Lexi clung to me tightly as I kissed and sucked on her hardened nipples, eliciting moans from her lips and frenzied gyrating against my length. The continual friction of her wetness against me made me harder than I had ever been. When my mouth finally found hers again, it was hot against mine, her kisses matching the intensity of my desire.

"Satisfy my pain," I murmured against her lips.

Lexi bit her lip as she looked into my eyes. I traced my hands up the soft skin of her back and reveled in the way she shivered under my touch.

Reaching down between us, she slowly eased me inside her warm body. A moan escaped her lips as she arched her back, drawing me further in.

My hold on her hips tightened, and she began to move, her hips grinding in small circles. My eyes were locked onto hers and it was glazed with lust.

I cupped her breasts, fingers lightly pinching and rolling her hard nipples. Lexi moaned, throwing her head back as she rode me harder. Her hands came up to grip my shoulders, using them for leverage as she bounced up and down on my length.

My gaze fell upon her swollen lips, the flush painting her cheeks, her braids wild and loose around her shoulders. She was a vision of wanton desire, all for me. My chest tightened with a possessive streak I hadn't known existed within me.

Holding onto her hips tighter, I rammed into her with vigor. My desire for her was unlike any I had known before. Suddenly, her movements grew more frantic, her breaths coming in pants and small grunts as she pleasured herself with my body. She was hot and unashamed, riding me with abandon.

"Marc," she whimpered, fingers digging into my shoulders.

At her call, I sat up slightly, wrapping my arm around her waist to pull her closer against me. I took a hardened nipple into my mouth, flicking it with my tongue as I drove into her harder, deeper, matching her frantic pace. Her name fell from my lips in a ragged groan, my breath hot against her skin.

It wasn't long before I felt the familiar tightening sensation, my body coursing with raw, primal pleasure. Her hot walls clamped tightly around me as she cried out my name.

Driving my pace to a frenzied peak, I growled out my release, shooting myself deep within her warmth.

We clung to each other, our breaths ragged and hearts pounding in sync. Lexi's body trembled against mine, her face buried in the crook of my neck. I held her close, savoring the feel of her soft curves molded against me.

As our breathing slowed, I eased us down onto the bed, Lexi's body still draped over mine. She lifted her head, her dark eyes meeting mine with a tender vulnerability.

"You're incredible," I whispered.

Lexi's lips curved into a soft smile, her fingers tracing idle patterns on my chest. "So are you," she whispered, her gaze holding mine.

Contentment washed over me, a sense of rightness I had never experienced before. Holding Lexi in my arms, our bodies still joined, I realized I wanted more than just stolen moments and secret rendezvous. I wanted her, all of her, in every way possible.

Lexi must have sensed the shift in my mood because she tilted her head, studying my face with a questioning look. "What are you thinking about?" she asked.

I hesitated, unsure how to put my feelings into words. I had never been one for grand declarations or sentimental speeches. But with Lexi, I felt a desire to be open, to let her see the parts of me I usually kept hidden.

"I'm thinking about how much I enjoy being with you," I said finally, my thumb stroking the soft skin of her cheek. "Not just like this, but talking to you, laughing with you, experiencing new things together."

She leaned into my touch, her lips brushing against my palm. "I feel the same way," she admitted. "Being with you feels...right. Like I'm exactly where I'm supposed to be."

My heart swelled at her words, a warmth spreading through my chest. I pulled her closer, capturing her lips in a slow, deep kiss. Lexi melted into me, her fingers threading through my hair as she returned the kiss with equal fervor.

When we finally broke apart, I rested my forehead against hers, our breaths mingling in the scant space between us. "Stay with me tonight," I said, my arms tightening around her waist.

"There's nowhere else I'd rather be," she whispered.

We spent the rest of the night wrapped in each other's arms, talking and laughing in hushed tones, stealing kisses and gentle caresses. As dawn approached, Lexi drifted off to sleep, her head pillowed on my chest and her body curled against mine.

I watched her sleep, knowing our connection was more than a fleeting vacation fling. It was deeper, real and precious.

Lexi

My heart fluttered when I spotted Marcus waiting for me at our usual café rendezvous point. Just the sight of his tall frame and devastating smile made my knees weak. I quickened my pace, giddy at the thought of feeling his arms around me again.

Yet as I drew close, a familiar heaviness settled in my chest. The thought of our inevitable goodbye lingered, quietly gnawing at the edges of my mind.

I couldn't let him see how much it was affecting me. I needed to keep it together, to savor the time we had left.

I pasted a smile on my face as Marcus pulled me in for a deep, hungry kiss. But as our lips parted, melancholy suffused me once more.

"What's wrong?" Marcus asked, his brows drawing together in concern.

I shook my head, trying to clear the gloomy thoughts. "It's nothing, just tired," I said, forcing a smile.

How could I voice my inner turmoil? That with each secret rendezvous, each passionate encounter, I was falling deeper in love with him.

A love with no future because our lives were anchored across the globe from each other. Marcus himself had said several times he didn't do long-term relationships.

As we strolled hand in hand through the lively piazza, my thoughts spiraled. In a few short days, this magical escape would end. I'd be on a plane home, leaving my heart behind with Marcus.

I pictured returning to my regular life—the hospital, my little apartment, evenings alone with my dogs. It would all feel empty now, devoid of joy and purpose. A future without Marcus seemed cold and bleak.

I would never again experience the thrill of his touch, the comfort of his arms. Never gaze into those intense dark eyes. My heart physically ached at the thought.

Marcus gently tilted my chin up, his brow furrowing. "Where did you go just now? You're a million miles away."

My eyes prickled with tears at losing Marcus when I had no claim on him. "Just thinking about everything I'll miss about Capri," I said.

It was the closest to the truth I could offer. I wouldn't burden him with my sadness when we were supposed to be enjoying these last few days together.

He studied my face intently before pulling me into another searing kiss. I closed my eyes and sipped the sweet wine of the moment.

His arms tightened around me as if he were trying to commit every detail of me to memory. I let myself sink into his warmth, wishing I could pause this moment forever.

But the sand was slipping too quickly through the hourglass. Soon our secret haven would be a memory, distant as the sea.

"Did you really go to the Grotto?" Hazel asked me hours later while the group sat on deck chairs, laughing and talking. The older children were tanned, happy, and playing in the pool under the watchful eyes of Marcus Sr. and Robyn, while the nannies kept the babies entertained.

I smiled absently, nodding in reply. My mind was still on those stolen moments with Marcus. I forced a laugh and joined the lighthearted conversation about our adventures in Capri.

"I did," I said, feigning enthusiasm. "The water was so blue and clear. Straight out of a dream." I didn't mention Marcus' accompaniment and the intimate moments we shared underwater.

Hazel grinned, her eyes lighting up with wanderlust. "I can't wait to see it one day."

My smile faltered when my gaze landed on Marcus across the pool, chatting with the others. He looked content, happy even, while my heart pounded with an ache only I understood.

Amy spoke next. "Tell me all those days you've been disappearing on your own, you haven't been exploring solo!" She grinned at the other girls, seeking their moral support. "We have seen very little of you on this trip. Are you sure you haven't been sneaking off for an assignation with some Italian stallion?"

Hazel gasped as I colored up. "You have, haven't you!" She looked around at the other women in delight. "Sneaky Lexi here has been hiding a European beau!"

There were sounds of excitement all around, with high-fives and squeals, as the women pounced on the idea. I studiously avoided looking in Marcus's direction.

He would definitely be watching me with amusement. Only we knew my stallion was American and brown-skinned.

Kneshel cut in. "Lexi is engaged. She wouldn't sneak off to meet some random."

There was a moment of silence as they all turned to me. "Really?" Trina asked, practically bug-eyed. "You're getting married?"

Amy asked, "You and Ben are making it official? He never mentioned it."

Amy and Ben worked at the Valleyfield fire station together. She was a paramedic and Ben a firefighter.

"I had no idea!" Marlowe exclaimed.

I squirmed in my seat and mumbled sheepishly, "Well, I didn't say anything because we... Ben and I... decided to keep everything low-key for now. His mom's ill, so... we're focusing on her comfort right now."

I gave Kneshel a side-eye. *Why did she have to open her big mouth?* Especially in present company.

Kneshel read the look and apologized, but also added defensively, "It was going to come out, anyway. You'll eventually get married!"

I could hear and almost feel the cold steel in Marcus's voice as he entered the conversation. "I wasn't aware you were engaged, Lexi." His casualness was a mockery noticeable only by me.

I nodded miserably, and he continued. "Congratulations. How long?"

"Not long," I mumbled, still unable to look at him.

Kneshel had no qualms about filling in the blanks. "Ben and Lex have been dating since Christmas, and two weeks ago he popped the question in his childhood home. The house where they fell in love."

There was a collective awww. Trina demanded pictures, but I cringed on the inside.

In truth, there'd never actually been a proposal. I put up my hands before myself as if the questions had turned into snowballs and got to my feet.

"I, um, have to...to...get ready for the beach."

My fervent wish was for Marcus to follow me. It was necessary for me to clarify things for him. I could only imagine what he must be thinking and feeling.

As I backed away, I heard Hazel's jovial rejoinder, "At least now we know you aren't sneaking off to meet Leonardo down on the beach!" The other women found her quip hilarious; I didn't crack a smile.

I froze as Marcus entered my cabin mere minutes after I did, carefully closing the door behind him. His jaw was clenched, his movements controlled and deliberate. But it was his cold eyes that sent a chill through me.

"You lied to me," he said evenly. Too evenly.

My mouth went dry. He was referring to our first meeting on Valentine's Day when he'd asked if I was single.

A knock at the door cut off any attempt to answer. I hurried to it, opening it just enough to stick my head through.

"I'm sorry. I did not know you and Ben didn't want to go public yet." Kneshel clapped her hands over her cheeks. "Can you forgive me? I hope I didn't make things awkward for you!"

"It's fine," I responded, because Kneshel seemed upset over her gaffe. "Don't worry about it," I said hastily, hoping Kneshel would get the message and leave. I could feel the brooding pressure of Marcus's presence behind me.

Kneshel frowned a little as she searched my face with concern, but then nodded and backed off. "Alright."

As soon as the other woman disappeared up the corridor, I turned back to the seething man standing in my room.

"My relationship with Ben..."

Marcus held up a hand, silencing me. "Don't. I know what you're going to say. More lies and excuses."

His voice remained a mask of icy calm, but there was contempt in his words that cut me deeply. This cold, detached anger was somehow worse than yelling.

"I asked you point-blank if you were involved with anyone," he went on. "You looked me in the eye and said you weren't."

I shook my head helplessly. "I'm sorry," I whispered, my hands trembling at my sides.

I wanted to explain everything, but the words wouldn't come. Marcus's coldness left me frozen, unsure of how to reach him. I needed to stay calm, to find the right words, but all I could manage in the moment was an apology.

"Sorry about what, exactly? Lying to me, or using me to turn your fiancé," he spat out the word, "into a cuck?"

"Marcus..." I stopped. How could I possibly respond to his allegations? "Ben and I are...." I began.

"You made a fool of me," Marcus interrupted, still eerily composed. Only the muscle feathering along his jawline gave away his rage.

My eyes filled with tears. I reached for him, but he evaded my touch, withdrawing into himself like a fortress.

"You live in Valleyfield," he interrupted me. "You know my mother's history, correct?"

I nodded mutely. Everyone in town knew that Simone Davis had run off with her married lover, Thomas Wesson, leaving her bewildered husband behind.

Her body and that of her lover's had been recovered over six years ago. The runaway couple had been deceased for almost the entirety of their disappearance.

"My mother was a cheat and a liar, and she hurt my father, and us, with her actions." His eyes were almost black when they settled on mine. "Duplicity is something I have zero tolerance for, Lexi."

His words echoed around the room as I stood there, frozen under his gaze. Each icy word was an arrow to my heart.

I longed to tell him the truth, but his detached fury left no room for an explanation. I swallowed hard, tears streaming down my face unabated. This was not how I'd imagined my vacation ending.

"Please, let me explain."

"Explain?" He scoffed, shaking his head. "The time for explanations is past, Lexi," he said bluntly. "I believed myself in lo..." He shook his head again. "My mistake."

Jaw set, Marcus turned on his heel and strode for the door. He paused with his hand on the knob, looking back at me one last time, eyes inscrutable.

"I don't give second chances."

The click of the door closing rang with dreadful finality. I collapsed onto the bed, sobbing. I should have told him everything before now. If I had, he wouldn't be hurting and believing me to be deceitful.

The sound of tapping on my door interrupted my pity-fest. I didn't dare hope Marcus was on the other side, and I was right not to. It was Kneshel, her face creased with concern.

"Are you alright? You're crying!" With smooth, practiced motions, Kneshel pressed the back of her hand against my forehead, grabbed my wrist and checked my pulse. "You aren't sick, are you?"

I shook my head, and once I got my hand back, I led Kneshel over to the tiny round table flanked by two chairs and motioned for her to sit.

"I have been meeting someone on the island. A man."

Kneshel stared at me, completely at a loss for words.

I took a breath and plunged. "Marcus..."

Kneshel was so stunned she asked idiotically, "Am I supposed to know him?"

I threw up my hands in frustration. "Marcus Davis Junior... MJ!"

Kneshel's eyes widened, and she gasped. "Oh, Lexi. Why didn't you tell me?"

"I..." I struggled for words. "I wanted to keep it private."

Kneshel took my hand, her usual fun-loving demeanor replaced by one of fierce protectiveness. "What about Ben?"

"You know Aunt Sheryl's ill. But what I didn't mention was..." I began, and for the next several minutes poured my heart out to Kneshel, explaining the arrangement between myself and Ben. I explained that while I loved Ben, I wasn't in love with him. "I'm in love with Marcus, but now he hates me."

Kneshel clapped her hand over her mouth. "Because I let the cat out of the bag!"

"No," I insisted, gripping Kneshel's hands tightly. "It's not your fault. All of this... it's on me, for not telling Marcus the truth from the beginning."

Kneshel's brows knitted in concern. "But how could you have known? You barely knew MJ. And by your own admission, this fling with him was supposed to be temporary."

"True," I admitted, "But... I fell in love with him, Kneshel. I fell for him harder and faster than I ever thought possible, and now... now he thinks I'm just like his mother."

Kneshel frowned, a cloud of worry crossing her features. "That's not a fair comparison, Lexi."

"But Marcus doesn't see it that way," I said, fresh tears welling in my eyes. "He told me he doesn't give second chances. And why should he? After what his mother did to his family..."

Kneshel squeezed my hand reassuringly. "Lexi, don't do this to yourself," she said. "I'm going to give you the same advice you gave me two years ago when I believed things were over with Lamont. Give it time." She touched my hand lightly, adding, "MJ is angry right now, but he'll calm down. And when he does, explain everything and tell him how you feel about him."

That may be true, but I didn't have the luxury of time. We were scheduled to return to the States in less than forty-eight hours. And Marcus lived in Asia.

Once Kneshel left, her words processed in my mind. She was right. I couldn't let Marcus walk away without knowing the truth.

I owed him that much, at least. He deserved to understand everything about Ben, me and my feelings for him. Even if he didn't forgive me, I needed to make things right, if only to ease the hurt I'd caused him.

I got up and stood in front of the mirror. My hands trembling as I washed my face and reapplied my lipstick. My mind raced with everything I wanted to say to Marcus, but the words felt heavy, uncertain.

What if he wouldn't listen? What if this was already over?

I had to try, but the thought of facing him again sent a wave of anxiety through me. Still, I couldn't leave things like this.

Taking a deep breath, I made my way to his cabin, my heart pounding with every step.

MJ

I could barely see my way to my cabin, overwhelmed by emotion. Storming off wasn't my style. I was usually composed. But Lexi's dishonesty had pushed me past my breaking point. My chest felt hollow, like my soul had been ripped apart.

Once inside, I sat on the edge of the bed, my mind racing. I couldn't let this break me. Lexi had blindsided me, but I wasn't someone who stayed down for long. I needed to clear my head, figure out my next move, and regain control. Letting my emotions spiral was not an option.

My eyes landed on the Visconti fountain pen resting on the nightstand. Lexi had bought it in town and gifted it to me with a shy smile.

"A memento, to thank you for making my first vacation the best," she had said.

I picked up the pen and, without thinking, hurled it across the room. It bounced off the wall and hit the floor with a hollow thud.

This was supposed to be a fun, temporary fling. How had I let my guard down enough to get hurt?

I replayed every conversation, every touch, every laugh. I knew now it was all lies.

The room felt smaller, the walls closing in. With a frustrated curse, I shot up from the bed and stormed out, my footsteps echoing on the polished wood floors. I needed air. I needed to think.

I found myself at the stern of the yacht, leaning against the railing, looking out at the gentle, blue waves. It was contradictory to my churning mind and stormy heart.

I tried to find solace in the steady rhythm of the waves, the way they danced under the sunlight, but all I could see was Lexi's sparkling eyes reflecting in them. The wind caressed my face with a cool touch, as if trying to soothe my burning anger and pain.

My fists tightened around the cool metal of the railing as I closed my eyes, letting the salt-kissed wind whip through my hair. A single tear traced down my cheek, lost in the whiskers of my unshaven face. I was a sturdy oak tree amid a hurricane, standing strong but being ravaged from within.

I exhaled, realizing I'd been holding my breath. My grip on the railing loosened slightly as astonishment washed over me. My heart felt heavy, weighed down with regret. But more at myself than at her.

How had I let Lexi's lie hit me this hard? A humorless laugh escaped my lips, swallowed by the vastness of the ocean stretching out before me.

As I stood there, staring at the endless horizon, I made a vow: never again would I let someone get close enough to wreak this kind of havoc on my heart. With that decision made, I pulled my gaze from the water and headed for the upper deck. I needed a drink or five.

When I arrived, I saw my dad and Robyn playing with a few of the kids. I would've preferred to be alone, but there wasn't much I could do about that. I scanned the bar, considering my options, when I sensed my father's presence beside me.

"I'm guessing you didn't know the young lady was engaged," he said quietly.

I turned, startled by his directness. So, he had known.

His eyes moved over my face, reading me easily. "Don't look so surprised. I've seen the two of you leaving the boat separately but returning together. About a week ago, I noticed you leaving the café near the harbor. And I've seen Lexi sneaking out of your cabin at dawn these past few mornings."

I felt my face heat, just as it had when I'd been a teenager and my father called me out over some reckless mischief. "Why did you stay?" I asked, my voice steady but firm. "You knew she was cheating, and you stayed."

He didn't seem rattled by the question. Instead, he paused, as if considering it, then reached for a bottle of aged Scotch. Pouring a shot for each of us, he finally spoke.

"All I ever wanted was for your mom to love me the way I loved her. She was the love of my life, from the moment I saw her in middle school." He shrugged, a small, sad gesture. "And it's how I was raised. Marriage was for life. You took the good with the bad. Leaving was never an option for me... even though it was for her in the end."

After mom disappeared with her lover, dad filed a wrongful death lawsuit against Thomas's wife, convinced that Deidre Wesson had killed her husband and my mother. But Deidre had airtight proof—bank statements and ATM footage from Tijuana proving her husband was still alive. Forced to drop the case, my father seemed to shrink into himself, becoming a shell of the man I once knew.

Years passed without a word from the couple until detectives showed up at my father's door. They had found skeletal remains in a car hanging off a cliff. The identification at the scene listed my mother and Thomas. Dental records confirmed their identities.

Regret tightened my chest whenever I thought of my mother's final moments. I remembered her smiling face and kind eyes looking at me with love and pride.

But the last time I saw her, the light had dimmed. Our final conversation had been a bitter exchange, hateful words thrown in anger. When I left for college, I had cut her out of my life.

Now, I would never hear her voice again. Never get the chance to apologize, to make amends for my cruelty. She died believing her only son hated her, when in truth, beneath my pride, I had always loved her.

"It must have been hard, staying loyal to her after everything she put you through." More bluntly, I added, "But you should have left. There's no excuse for infidelity."

I wasn't just talking about my mother. I hated lies and cheating, and there was no way I could tolerate that from anyone.

"I stayed for the family," my father said quietly. "I wanted you kids to grow up in a stable, loving home."

"It didn't work out the way you hoped," I shot back, the frustration clear in my voice. "Maybe we would have been better off with happy co-parents instead."

He rested a hand on my arm and gave it a gentle squeeze. "I don't regret the life we had. And I wouldn't change a thing, because if I had, Hazel might not exist. Hell, maybe you wouldn't either."

As his words hung in the air between us, I felt a sudden surge of understanding. It wasn't that my father had been blind to my mother's faults or her infidelity. He had known, but he'd made a deliberate choice to stay. For his kids.

"I take it things didn't end well with Lexi?" he asked gently.

I shook my head.

"Don't let the mistakes your mother and I made get between you and Lexi," he continued. "I've seen the way she looks at you when she thinks no one is watching. She loves you." He took a thoughtful sip of his drink. "I don't know what's going on with her and this fiancé, but if she's not being honest about it, that tells you something about how she feels."

I wanted to protest, but my dad held up a hand.

"Hear me out. I know you've seen relationships fall apart, and it's made you wary. When your mother left, I was angry too. Angry at her, at myself. I felt like a fool." He gazed out at the waves. "For a long time, I told myself I was better off alone. But you know what it cost me? Years wasted on loneliness and regret. I missed out on so much joy and caused your sisters pain."

Shaking his head as if to rid himself of his thoughts, my father turned to me. "I stayed with your mother too long, but don't make the opposite mistake. Don't walk away too quickly from someone you care about without knowing everything."

His dad clasped his shoulder. "It's your choice, son. But sometimes forgiveness requires great courage. Don't let your pride make a decision you'll come to regret."

I turned my dad's words over in my mind as I stared down into my glass. Maybe Lexi deserved a chance to explain her side of things.

Was I ready to lose her, to go back to my routine life as if she'd never existed? I let out a sigh and downed my scotch in one swift gulp.

I made the decision then and there. I would walk away. It wasn't just about the betrayal; it was about self-preservation. I wasn't the type to stay in a situation that didn't serve me. If Lexi couldn't be honest with me, then she wasn't worth the risk.

But how would I avoid her on this yacht? I would likely encounter her again, and I didn't want to. I wasn't my father. I refused to be taken in by a pretty face and lying tongue.

The thought of seeing her again was as painful as the possibility that I never might. Twenty minutes later, I was back in my cabin, surrounded by my sisters, who were loudly protesting my announced departure, even as I hastily shoved my belongings into my bags.

"Can't you leave tomorrow?" Trina asked.

"I told you," I answered regretfully, hating to do this to them, but my mind was made. "It's urgent. I'm needed back at the office. I really have to go."

Looking at their crestfallen faces, I almost changed my mind, but stayed the course. Spotting the pen I'd flung away earlier, I picked it up and placed it in my bag, zipping it shut.

"I'm going to miss you," Hazel said, her face looking like she was still trying to grapple with the sudden change of plans.

"I'll miss you too," I replied, pulling both her and Trina into a quick hug.

By the time I made it upstairs to say my goodbyes to the rest of my family, I felt hollow.

"Take care of yourself," my father said gruffly, as we hugged tightly. His voice wavered slightly, and he cleared his throat, but didn't pull away immediately. "She's not married yet, and as long as she isn't, she's fair game."

His words echoed in my mind. But I had already decided. I would not be like my namesake. I would not stay when I should leave.

Just as I stepped out of my father's embrace, I heard a soft voice calling out my name. I froze, my heart pounding as I turned slowly to see Lexi standing there in a flowing floral dress. The hem brushed against her ankles with every gust of wind.

Our eyes met, and for a moment, it felt like we were the only two people in the world. The sorrow and longing in Lexi's gaze sent my heart racing, urging me to go to her. But I forced myself to resist.

"Marcus," Lexi pleaded, taking a step toward me. "Don't leave yet. Not like this."

My sisters and their friends stopped what they were doing to watch the unfolding drama. Behind me, Trina drew in a soft gasp.

I could imagine her wide-eyed glance at Hazel as understanding dawned about me and Lexi. On the periphery, I noticed their friends leaning in, riveted by the scene.

I was tempted to cross the distance between us, to wipe away the tears glistening her cheeks, but I stood rooted to the spot. As much as it shredded me inside, I had to protect myself.

"No," I said firmly.

Every part of me wanted to go to her, to erase the pain in her eyes, but I couldn't. I had to protect myself, and it meant walking away. "This is over, Lexi."

And with that, I turned and walked away, each step taking me farther from the woman who had unexpectedly captured my heart. I didn't look back, refusing to allow myself one last glimpse. What we'd had was over. It was time to close this chapter and move on.

Hours later, I settled into my spacious first-class seat, but my mind was far from settled. As the plane climbed to cruising altitude, I opened my laptop, determined to focus on work. My latest legal brief stared back at me from the screen, rows of clinical black text. I read the same paragraph three times, but the words blurred together.

With a frustrated sigh, I leaned back and closed my eyes. Behind my eyelids, unbidden images of Lexi flashed. Her radiant smile, the brush of her fingers against my cheek, the kisses we shared in the piazza. Laughing together over gelato. The passion in her eyes whenever I sheathed myself inside her. The pain in her eyes when I finally walked away...

My hands clenched on the armrests and I willed myself to stop replaying those moments. It was over now. A clean break now was better than getting in too deep.

A flight attendant stopped by, offering a drink. I accepted it, my mind already shifting gears. I needed to focus on work and on my future.

Letting my emotions get the best of me wasn't an option. I stared out the window into the endless night sky, reminding myself of what really mattered. I wouldn't let this derail me.

Lexi

I sat in Aunt Sheryl's backyard, my eyes landing on the drooping daisies and overgrown rose bushes that had once been Aunt Sheryl's pride and joy. Now they stood neglected, mourning the loss of the woman who had nurtured them for years.

When she became ill, the garden suffered, despite our—Ben, Tiffany, and my—attempts to take up some of the slack. And now, Aunt Sheryl would never again plunge her hands into the rich earth, or boast about how her daffodils were coming along. It was a tragedy.

A lump formed in my throat as I thought about how vibrant and full of life Aunt Sheryl used to be. She would never bake her famous cinnamon buns for the church fundraisers again or regale everyone with funny stories from her youth. A vital part of the community was gone, leaving an emptiness that could never be filled.

I blinked rapidly, willing the tears to stay at bay, but the weight of grief pressed down on me, making it hard to breathe. Aunt Sheryl had been a second mother to me since my own parents died. Her passing reopened that wound.

Why did the people I loved keep getting taken away?

Marcus... I hadn't allowed myself to think about him too much, but even now, two months later, the pain of losing him felt fresh, like a wound I couldn't quite heal. I had to be careful, though.

I couldn't let myself spiral into what-ifs and regrets. It wouldn't change anything. He was gone, and no amount of wishing could bring him back.

"Hey," Ben said from behind me.

"It was a beautiful funeral," I told him, picturing the profusion of lilies surrounding Aunt Sheryl's casket.

The wooden bench creaked as Ben's sturdy frame settled beside me. His strong hands squeezed my shoulders, pulled me closer, his warmth comforting and familiar.

Aunt Sheryl had been his mom, and him, her only son. I glanced at Ben, trying to gauge how he was holding up.

He'd always been the strong one, the one who kept it together for everyone else, but I knew the depth of his pain. I rested my hand on his arm, offering silent comfort. He talked little about his feelings, but I could sense the weight of his grief, heavier than mine.

"Mom planned it all out in her last days," Ben said.

Aunt Sheryl's foresight and strength in planning her own funeral in her final days was both inspiring and heartbreaking. She didn't want her transition to burden us.

"I really hate to do this to you," Ben began. "But I can't marry you. I mean, you're hot and smart and hot," Ben continued, the hint of a smile touching his lips, "but I could never marry a woman who's in love with another man."

I sucked my teeth in an amused dismissal of his ridiculous comment. "You are full of it."

"Seriously, though, thanks for participating in this scheme. Mom spent her final days at peace, believing I would be well looked after, loved and cared for. She went to her rest thinking that her best friend's lovely daughter held my heart in her hands, and would never let me go." He gave me a sad smile. "She died happy."

I nodded, emotion constricting my throat. "I know. But there will be repercussions from her in the afterlife. You know that, right?" I didn't want to think about what this fake engagement had cost me.

"Yep! But hopefully neither of us will have to face her wrath anytime soon." We both chuckled. "Can I do anything to fix this rift between you and MJ? I could explain things."

I shook my head quickly. "No. There's nothing to fix, Ben. It's done." My voice came out sharper than I intended, and I forced myself to soften. "Even if you explained, it wouldn't change any-thing."

I pictured Marcus's handsome face, his warm eyes and tender smile. My heart clenched with loss. I would move on eventually, I told myself. I had to.

Over the next several weeks, I allowed my routine to swallow me up. Work, home, walk my dogs. Work, home, walk my dogs. It helped numb the pain of loss and chase away thoughts of Marcus.

When I saw his family, I ducked and dodge. Hazel called out to me once, and I pretended to not hear. I avoided shopping at Wessonmart during the day to avoid Hazel, who seemed intent on making it a habit to call on me and greet me with hugs like we were family.

It was dark and almost closing time at Wessonmart when another cart bumped into mine. I was on the verge of apologizing when I looked up and saw Marcus Sr. smiling at me.

"Hi, Lexi. What a pleasant surprise!"

"Hello." I smiled back at him, the expression feeling brittle on my lips.

I attempted to maneuver my cart away, the metal creaking as I turned it. I couldn't bear to keep looking into his kind, familiar face. It was like seeing a faded photocopy of his son, whose charming image still tortured my every waking moment.

Marcus Sr. grasped my arm, his warm fingers curling around my wrist. "I haven't seen you around much since we got back from vacation. Why don't you join us for Sunday dinner this weekend? Robyn and I host the family every second Sunday."

Heat flooded my cheeks at his words. Marcus's family had been nothing but kind to me, and yet here I was, hiding from them, avoiding any reminders of what I'd lost.

"Thank you for the invitation, sir," I said softly. "But I already have plans this Sunday." The lie tasted bitter on my tongue.

I remembered how Marcus's sisters and Robyn had comforted me after his abrupt departure from the yacht. I recalled the gentle weight of Hazel's hand on my shoulder and Trina's comforting words as they'd enveloped me in hugs.

None of them had accused me of inappropriate behavior. Instead, they'd radiated shock and then joy when in my moment of vulnerability admitted my deep feelings for Marcus to them.

Later, after Marcus Senior and Robyn had retired for the evening, all the women had clustered together on the moonlit deck. As they sipped cocktails, they'd recounted the boundaries they pushed and the romantic risks they'd taken to now have the happy marriages they cherished.

Trina and Joy's stories had been the most affecting. Forbidden royal romance and murder-for-hire plots were always the most intriguing stories.

Marcus Sr. released my arm, and my mind returned to the present. "Another time then," he said, giving me a knowing look.

Before I could respond, he scribbled something on a receipt and pressed it into my palm. With a final pat on my hand, Marcus steered his cart down the aisle, leaving me staring after him.

I unwrapped the folded slip with trembling fingers, gasping softly as I read an address in Singapore and an international phone number. My heart stuttered in my chest. The senior Marcus had given me a way to contact Marcus.

My mind raced, my thoughts tripping over themselves. Should I call him? Just show up on his doorstep unannounced?

The thought alone made my pulse race, but I couldn't act on impulse. What if he didn't want to see me? Or worse, what if I made things more complicated by showing up?

I had to think this through. I couldn't afford to make another mistake.

When I opened my front door that night, I braced for the usual enthusiastic greeting by Kung and Fu. They yapped around my ankles, shoving each other aside as they competed for my attention.

I dropped to my knees, laughing as I opened my arms to them, hugging each. "Yes, I brought treats," I said to Kung as he shoved his face into one of my reusable shopping bags. "But no, you can't have any until after dinner."

Even as they pouted, I pulled out the ingredients I'd bought and waved them. "I got strip steak and a fresh hunk of cheddar. And we have rice and broccoli. Dinner's going to be good!"

I set about cooking dinner for my precious pups. They ate better than many humans, but it couldn't be helped. Dry dog food was not it.

As the rice and cheese dish simmered on the stove, my doorbell rang, and in sailed Tiffany with my niece and nephew, seconds later. I was certain that my niece rang the doorbell, since my sister normally let herself in with her key. After the flurry of hugs, the kids ran off to the living room to play with the dogs, leaving the two of us alone.

"Smells good," Tiffany commented, peeking into the pot on the stove. "Is there enough for all of us?"

I laughed. "Nope. Cooked enough for just myself, Kung, and Fu."

"Girl, you need to have kids. That's what you need. Cooking up gourmet meals for dogs. I could never!"

We'd had that argument before, so I didn't bother to respond. Instead, I asked, "What brings you by?"

"I haven't seen much of you since you recently." She grinned at me. "I figured I'd come over and see for myself you're okay."

I felt guilty for neglecting Tiffany these past few weeks. "I'm sorry I've been distant lately. With Aunt Sheryl... and everything else, I just... needed some time." I reached out, giving her hand a squeeze.

Tiffany was immediately understanding. "I miss her. It's hard to accept she's not a phone call away." She shook her head. "She'll miss your wedding."

My heart sank. I'd forgotten to update Tiffany on my and Ben's fake engagement.

I set two glasses down on the table, reached into my cabinet for the bottle of limoncello I'd brought back from Italy, and said, "I have something to tell you..."

I spent the next hour coming clean to my sister, explaining the fake engagement and my whirlwind romance with Marcus. I left out the more intimate details of our time together.

As close as we were, we never discussed our sex lives. Tiffany still viewed me as her innocent baby sister, and I respected those boundaries.

Tiffany listened intently, her dark eyes growing wider and wider. When I finally finished, she was stunned into silence. Then her eyebrows drew together.

"You and Ben didn't need to go through all that pretense!" she burst out. "Aunt Sheryl would've been fine without the lie."

I dropped my gaze, chastened. "I know, but... I wanted to make her happy. And Ben is my best friend."

Guilt squeezed my heart in an iron fist. I should have been honest with my sister and... Marcus from the start.

Tiffany exhaled heavily, the lemon scent of her breath wafting over me. Her expression softened. "I know you meant well, sis. No more secrets between us from now on. Deal?"

I met her stern but caring look. "Deal."

"Now tell me more about you and MJ. You know he graduated high school with Allan?" I hadn't known that, and as the limoncello disappeared between us, I smiled through bittersweet tears. It felt cathartic to talk things over with Tiffany.

Over the next couple of days, I replayed the conversation in my mind. Tiffany's insistence that I fly to Singapore to reconcile with Marcus kept echoing through my thoughts.

Could I fly to Asia and throw myself at his feet? Maybe I should save myself the embarrassment and write him a letter...

I looked up flights to Singapore on my phone. I tried not to cringe at the cost for flight and hotel. Because of Aunt Sheryl's 50-30-20 rule about money management, I was intentional about how I spent my money.

Fifty percent of my salary went towards my needs, thirty percent went to my wants, and the remaining twenty went into savings.

Though during certain months, I added thirty percent to my savings. Visiting Marcus, in my opinion, was both a need and a want.

By the time the weekend came, I was bursting with anxious energy. I needed a distraction and pizza. Comfort food, my girls, and *Sundance Beach* would provide a momentary escape. Judging from the trailers, *Sundance Beach* promised to be filled with breakups, makeups, and new secrets.

"Pizza incoming!" I called out as I plunked down the boxes, pushing aside my nerves for the evening. The exhilarating, terrifying possibility of seeing Marcus again consumed me.

My impulsive trip to Singapore was scheduled for tomorrow evening, but tonight, Kneshel, Rilya, and Evie were all there. Their presence helped to calm my nerves over what awaited me on the other side of the world.

Possible rejection and humiliation.

Ben had turned up unexpectedly a few minutes ago and decided to stay. As I fussed with the refreshments, I amused myself by listening to him and Evie bicker on the couch. Evie had been looking forward to it being an all-girls hangout and had rolled her eyes when Ben sat down.

"Ugh! Why are you even here?" Evie asked, as she rolled her eyes.

Ben grabbed a handful of popcorn from the bowl on Evie's lap with a chuckle. "What? I can't watch *Sundance Beach* too?"

"As if!" Evie scoffed. "You're a guy! What would you know about it?"

"Oh yeah? Then who do you ship Gabby with, Aaron or Diego?" Ben challenged with a teasing glint in his eyes.

Evie shoved his shoulder playfully. "Everyone knows she belongs with Aaron! Diego is better suited for Mia." Moments later, Gabby and Aaron broke up yet again, causing Evie to sigh loudly. "These kids break up more often than I change clothes."

Ben chuckled. "That's really saying something coming from you, Evie."

Evie gasped and smacked Ben's arm. "What's that supposed to mean?"

"Are you and your boyfriend together or broken up these days?" Ben teased.

"None of your business!" Evie said.

Rilya, Kneshel, and I exchanged knowing looks. We all knew Evie was present tonight because she broke up with Darius earlier in the day. Darius had apparently taken too long to answer her texts the previous night.

The moment there was a commercial break, I rushed off to the bathroom, only to hear the chime of my doorbell. "Can someone get that?" I called out.

Seconds later, I heard excited chatter as the visitor was presumably ushered in. Probably Lamont, I figured. Hardly able to stay away from Kneshel for a heartbeat.

By the time I exited the bathroom, my guests were completely silent, which was worrying. Ben and Evie should be arguing.

"Why is it so quiet? Did I miss something?" I asked, while making my way to the living room.

I stopped dead. Kung and Fu were leaping around and yelping in excitement, angling for the attention of a man who was on his haunches petting them.

At the sound of my arrival, the man stood and turned around, pushing his glasses up on his face. *Marcus.*

"Your friends left," he announced, looking slightly sheepish. His arrival had apparently triggered the exodus.

I stood frozen in place, my brain struggling to make sense of his presence. How was he here? He wasn't supposed to be here.

My heart pounded, but I forced myself to stay still, unsure of how to react. I'd imagined seeing him again a thousand times, but now he was here, I didn't know what to say.

MJ

I had thought returning to Singapore would be what I needed to get Lexi out of my mind. I was wrong. Despite burying myself in work, fanciful images of her haunted my thoughts.

My penthouse began to feel unfamiliar, the skyline feeling like a cage of glass and steel. I realized no amount of distance could dull the ache taking root in my chest. Every luxury around me turned to ash, a bitter reminder that without her, I was merely existing, not living.

Being without her wasn't just unbearable, it was impossible. I couldn't function, couldn't focus, and every day without her felt like a waste.

There was only one solution: move back to Valleyfield and win her back. I wasn't interested in half measures. I was going all-in, and I wasn't backing down until she was mine.

My weekly phone calls with Dad were filled with subtle hints about Lexi. He kept bringing up how she looked alongside her fiancé, and my sisters never missed an opportunity to remind me of how foolish I was for not going after her. It was clear they had turned against me, and honestly, I couldn't blame them.

I could have easily asked one of my sisters for Lexi's number, but a phone call wasn't enough. I needed to see her in person, to hold her in my arms again.

As I moved toward her, uncertainty gnawed at me. What if she told me to leave?

But when our eyes locked, I knew coming here was the right decision. God, I had missed her. The last couple of months had felt like an eternity.

"You left without saying goodbye..." she murmured.

"I'm here now. And I'm not leaving until you're mine, Lexi. I've spent too much time without you already."

"I'm supposed to be on a flight to Singapore tomorrow," she said.

I couldn't suppress my surprise at her announcement. "You were coming after me?"

"I was afraid you'd ignore my calls, so I bought a ticket—"

Without hesitation, I pulled her into me, my arms wrapping around her to claim what was mine. This wasn't a simple kiss. I devoured her, letting her feel the intensity of everything I had held back for the past two months. She melted into me, and I knew she was mine.

Her rigid muscles relaxed as she melted into me. Her arms wrapped around my neck, and she pulled herself closer, allowing me to sweep her off her feet.

"I've been a fool," I confessed, pulling back enough to see her face. "A fool to let you go, and I've thought of nothing but you since we parted. I hate myself for not giving you a chance to talk."

"I should have told you about Ben and me," she began.

"Yes. But I shouldn't have turned my back on you that last time. I was the asshole who didn't let you speak. And I'm more like my mother than I thought because I don't care about your engagement. I want you anyway."

"Marcus—"

"I met Ben." I gestured backward at the closed door. "He seems like a stand-up guy, but he made a huge mistake leaving you alone with me. I'm declaring war, Lexi. I'm going to fight for your mind, your body, and your heart. I've moved back to Valleyfield to be with you."

When she gasped, I continued, "It's my mission from now on, whatever it takes. I'm in this for the long haul."

Tears gathered in her eyes and leaked down her cheek. I licked every salty drop. And instead of warning me off as I expected, she said, "You've already won, Marcus. All of me belongs to you."

My heart thumped wildly against my ribs as those simple yet powerful words echoed in my ears. Unspoken feelings, misinterpretations, and silent signals had created an expanse between us, a void now filled with her affirmation. I felt a sense of overwhelming relief sweep over me, washing away months of regret and self-loathing.

Without breaking eye contact, I leaned towards her. "Say it again," I pleaded in a whisper, needing to hear the words once more, to assure myself that I wasn't caught up in some precarious dream.

She held my gaze steadily, the corners of her lips turning upwards just slightly into a warm smile. "I'm yours, Marcus. Only yours."

I claimed her lips again with a hunger born from the painful weeks of separation. Every touch, every shared breath, felt like sweet redemption. I was home.

There was so much I wanted to tell her. I began with the obvious.

"I love you, Lexi," I said, pulling away just enough to look into her eyes. "I've loved you since the moment I saw you holding Knöelle in your arms, and I've been an idiot for not saying it sooner. But I'm saying it now, and I will not stop until you believe it."

Lexi's body wiggled against mine, and it was then I realized she was upright in my arms. "Let me down, Marcus."

I complied and lowered her feet to the ground, but my arm didn't leave her waist. She looked up at me, those dark eyes bright with a mix of emotions.

"I need to explain some things about my engagement."

I groaned. "I don't want to—"

"Sit, please, Marcus." She gestured to the couch. I obeyed, followed by Kung and Fu, leaping and yipping for my attention.

I cracked a joke, hoping to ease the tension growing in my chest since she stepped out of my arms without admitting her feelings for me. "I feel threatened by your deadly protectors."

In response to my tentative smile, Lexi laughed, reminding me of how much I loved her laughter. The woman I loved was smiling at me. Everything would be okay.

She sat next to me, twisting her body sideways to look me in the eye. I waited. Then she began a halting story about her mom's best friend and the best friend's son, Ben.

I felt my spine stiffen at the mention of the name, like a big dog smelling a rival nearby, but I remained silent, willing my poker face.

Lexi had mentioned Sheryl in the past, and I knew the woman had stepped into the role of protector, provider, and nurturer after her parents' tragic deaths. The woman's kindness and generosity had taken the pressure off Tiffany's shoulders. Lexi's sister was able to complete her studies in massage therapy and save enough to afford a two-bedroom apartment with her boyfriend, Allan.

"About a year ago, Aunt Sheryl was diagnosed with terminal cancer. It was a terrible shock, especially to Ben." She licked her lips. It must have been painful for Lexi too. I lifted her hand and placed a kiss on her knuckles.

"Aunt Sheryl's dearest wish was always for Ben and me to end up together. She thought my introversion and his extroversion was a match made in personality heaven." Lexi flushed. "We always protested. Ben and I weren't into each other. Then this past Christmas, I jokingly suggested to Ben us being a couple would be the perfect Christmas present for his mother. And instead of calling me crazy, he jumped on it." She didn't have more than a few months to live, so we agreed to become a couple for Sheryl's last days on earth.

Lexi's eyes misted over. "It tore me up inside to lie to everyone," she confessed. "Smiling through dinners and parties, keeping up the act, knowing Aunt Sheryl's time was short." Her voice grew thick with emotion. "But I kept reminding myself how happy Aunt Sheryl was. She spent the last two months of her life planning her funeral and our wedding. She opened a Pinterest account and pinned everything." Lexi chuckled. "The flowers, the cakes, the food, the shoes, dresses, hairstyles, makeup... She was over the moon. And that made it easier for Ben and me, knowing she focused on something other than her pain."

As Lexi continued to explain everything, I watched her face, drinking in every detail. Seeing the tears gather in her eyes, I felt a pang of regret. I had been consumed with hurt and anger and had failed to listen to her side of the story. I had cast her as the villain without knowing the facts.

"Aunt Sheryl passed away a month ago," she finished.

The guilt was overwhelming. I reached out and cupped her face, my thumb wiping away the tear tracks staining her cheeks. "I'm sorry," I murmured.

"I should've told you about this from the beginning... I just... I don't know..." Her voice trembled with unshed tears.

"Shh…" I tried to soothe her, pressing my lips to her forehead. "We both made mistakes. But it's not too late to set things right between us."

"But how can you know that? How can I trust you to not walk away and cast me in the same net as your mother?"

I moved closer. "You're right to be concerned. I handled things terribly before. But these past weeks have been torture without you. And if it's taught me anything, it's my mom wasn't a villain. She was a wonderful mother, but ruled by her heart, and did a terrible thing. It was unfortunate the terrible thing affected many. But we've thankfully all moved on."

"Marcus, I'm sorry," Lexi whispered.

I reached for her hands. "I've never felt this way about anyone, Lexi. Being apart from you made me realize how empty my life is without you in it."

My thumb traced soothing circles over her knuckles, her skin soft and warm beneath my touch. Lexi shivered.

"I know I have to earn back your trust," I said. "And I will. I'll spend every day proving to you I'm not going anywhere. You have my word, Lexi. I'm never walking away again. Whatever it takes, I'm here for the long run."

"I was willing to travel across the world for you," she breathed. "My feelings haven't changed. But I can't go through you shutting me out again."

My jaw clenched as the weight of her words settled in. "Leaving you like that... it was wrong. I've learned my lesson, Lexi. I promise, I'll never do it again."

I lifted her hands to my lips, pressing firm, deliberate kisses to her fingers. Each touch was a promise, a vow to never let her go again. I wasn't just showing her love; I was giving myself to her. Lexi was my future, and I would do whatever it took to keep her by my side.

I tipped her chin up, and our lips met. Her warmth, the taste of her was my sanctuary.

After a long, deep kiss, Lexi pulled away. "I love you."

"I love you too, Lexi. More than anything or anyone in this universe or the next."

She touched my cheek, her gaze searching mine. "You really do love me," she repeated, as if needing reassurance.

"I do," I affirmed.

Rising to her feet, Lexi took my hand and pulled me up with her. The dogs whined in protest, sensing our impending departure, but I was too lost in the depths of her eyes to offer them any consolation.

"Where are we going?" I asked, but I already knew the answer.

Wherever it was, we were going together. I wouldn't let her slip away again. Lexi would become my wife, and I would father her children. I would make sure of it.

She smiled in response, her hand tightening around mine, possessive and determined. When we entered her surprisingly large bedroom, I understood. We were about to celebrate in the sweetest way possible.

Epilogue

"This is ridiculous," I complained. "How long am I supposed to wear this blindfold?" It was Valentine's Day, one year later, and I was becoming impatient. I was strapped into the passenger seat of Marcus's SUV and did not know where we were headed.

"If I tell you, it will ruin the surprise," he said, then chuckled. He reached down and patted my knee.

As the car rolled along, I smiled to myself as I thought back over the incredible months with Marcus. We'd weathered misunderstandings and heartache to find our happiness. Now my love for him was stronger than ever.

I remembered the ache I'd felt thinking he was lost to me, and the leap of faith it had taken to buy a ticket to Singapore. The look in his eyes when he turned up at my door had banished any lingering doubts.

His willingness to listen, understand, and forgive had meant everything. He was my rock.

We'd gone to Singapore the next day. Marcus had convinced me to make use of my booking, and I had agreed. We'd spent a week exploring the city, getting lost in lush gardens, savoring exotic foods, wandering through ancient temples, and making love under the glow of the Singapore skyline.

I couldn't imagine facing life without him by my side. We fit like two souls meant to be together.

This past November, Montrose University corrected the error in their judgment and hired Marcus as a professor. Marcus started working at the university in January and had negotiated a higher salary than what they previously offered.

Trina and Hazel welcomed me into the family. For the first time since I'd moved out of Aunt Sheryl's house all those years ago,

I spent Thanksgiving with Marcus's family rather than with the Lewis's.

This year, there were plans to split the day between the two families. I had no plans for ever hosting Thanksgiving.

Tiffany, Allan, and the Lewis's loved Marcus. Lamont's mom even commented on Marcus being a good man, regardless of his older sister. Even though Agnis loved Kneshel, she still smarted over what she perceived as Trina's snub toward her son.

I sensed the car slowing and Marcus easing it to a stop. The engine rumbled into silence, and I heard Marcus unbuckle his seatbelt. He emerged from the vehicle, took a moment before he came around and opened my door. He reached out for me, guiding me carefully as I stepped out onto the uneven ground.

"Watch your step," he advised, as I put all my trust in him. His touch was reassuring and comforting.

The air was crisp and thick with the scent of pine trees. We were no longer in town, which meant we were on the outskirts of Valleyfield.

With a flourish, Marcus whipped off the blindfold.

I blinked against the brightness, taking in my surroundings. The afternoon sunlight slanted across the open plot of land, casting a golden glow over the scrubby winter-browned grass.

A light breeze stirred the empty branches of a lone oak tree in the center of the property, its gnarled limbs etched starkly against the blue sky. A large white tent sat in the middle of the land.

"We're home."

"But..." A part of my brain struggled to process what was happening, but then Marcus dropped before me on one knee and held up a box. Only then did the full impact of his gesture hit me.

"Lexi, will you make me your husband? And make this our forever home?"

Later, I would tell my family I'd screamed out a resounding "Yes!", but the truth was the word was trapped in my head because my joy made me speechless. All I could do was nod and throw myself onto him.

When he lifted me into his arms and twirled me around, I felt the hot tears trickle down my cheeks. He set me down and began kissing them away, but there was something I had to tell him.

"I'm pregnant!" I took his hand with the one now bearing his ring and pressed it against my flat stomach.

His face went still for a moment before a wide grin lit up his handsome features. He bent down and pressed his lips tenderly against my stomach. "Hello, there," he murmured, his voice thick with emotion.

When he looked up at me, his dark eyes were shining. The sight tugged painfully at my heart. "Lexi... I love you," he said, the words raw and heartfelt.

"I love you too, baby," I said, cradling his face in my hands as I leaned in to kiss him. His lips were warm, eager, yet there was an underlying tenderness.

Our lips parted reluctantly, and Marcus wrapped an arm around my shoulders, pulling me close against him as he pressed a soft kiss to the crown of my head. I nestled into his chest, listening to the steady thrumming of his heart under my ear.

We remained there for what felt like an endless moment, embraced in each other's arms on the land that would become our home and nurture our family. The sun set, painting the sky with hues of pinks and purples. As the first stars twinkled, I was certain it matched the sparkle in my eyes.

"Let me show you the inside of the tent."

Together, we walked to the tent, which was roomy on the inside. It was cooled and furnished with two folding chairs, a table, and a double-sized metal bed. "Everything we need for a night or two," he told me.

I stared at him in astonishment. "How did you...?" I asked, but he silenced me by taking me into his arms again.

"All I want to do is kiss you," he confessed. "Touch you. Hold you." He took my hand and ran his thumb along the back of the glittering ring. "Now and always."

He set me back against the bed, hands working to inch my skirt up to bare my belly. He pressed his lips against it, and then whispered, "Daddy loves you, but we're going to need you to pretend we aren't here for a while, okay? Because there are pleasurable things I want to do to your mommy!"

I pretended to protest but gave that up fast, because all I wanted was to seal our new commitment in the most delicious way possible.

He was already undressing me, but I wanted to be the one to look after him. I motioned for him to stop, and instead began undoing each button of his shirt, removing each garment, almost reverently, kissing every inch of revealed skin as I did.

Carefully, I removed his glasses and set them aside, then ran my fingers through his low-cut hair. *Maybe I'd be able to convince him to grow it out.* I loved how it felt.

Taking off his boxers, I leaned in and kissed the length of his erect member, causing him to release a soft exhale. I teased him with the thought of taking him all the way into my mouth before pulling back at the last second.

Instead, I pressed his shaft between my breasts, squeezing them tight around his heated flesh, allowing him to move his hips against the snug embrace in which I held him. I studied his face, taking in the half-closed eyes and parted lips.

My greatest delight came not from my stimulation but from the excitement I felt at bringing him pleasure. I dipped my head to flick my tongue at his tip.

"Are you trying to kill me?" he grunted, moving faster as the momentum built.

"Maybe," I teased.

"I can't think of a better way to die." But he had the strength to pull away, put his own release on hold as he completed the task he'd first set himself: getting me naked.

When I was bare, Marcus set me back against the crisp new sheets on the double bed, hoisted himself onto his elbows above me, and looked down into my eyes. My entire body was by now aflame, eager, opening for him. But he didn't move.

"What are you waiting for?" I asked, though not impatiently.

His smile was radiant. "Not waiting. Soaking you in. I want to inhale you and drag my tongue against your skin until you're all I taste."

He reached between my thighs, stroking, teasing, making a way for himself. Then, once he'd positioned himself, he slid into me, welcomed by my eager, aroused body.

He didn't move, not at first. "I want to live here," he confessed. "Inside of you. Bury myself deep and experience your wonder. I love you, Lexi. Always."

I looped my arms around his neck and urged him to move. "I love you too. Always have, always will." I lifted my hand to look once more at the ring he'd placed on my finger, admiring its brilliance.

Marcus was moving now, thrusting into me with long strokes. My body responded to his every thrust like a symphony of pleasure, and each caress was a note that built up to a crescendo. I arched up to meet him, the sweet pleasure of his thickness stretching me, making me see stars.

There was no holding back. The tent filled with the sounds of our desire; heavy breathing, skin slapping against skin, and the rhythmic creaking of the bed beneath us. Words slipped from our lips in heated whispers. Declarations of lust and passion fueled our feverish movements.

He changed angle suddenly, his tip hitting my g-spot, making me spin into oblivion. My body writhed beneath his as he continued to pound into me relentlessly. The pleasure was overwhelming, but I wanted more... needed more.

His hand slid from my hip up to my breast, and he lowered his face to my nipple. He flicked it with his tongue, sucking and nibbling. It sent a jolt of pleasure straight to the pit of my stomach, intensifying the sensation of him moving inside me.

My body was a limber arc under him, writhing in ecstasy as he hit every single spot that made me tremble. My nails dug into his back, marking him as mine.

"Marc," I moaned his name, voice shaking with the waves of pleasure flowing through my body.

Our rhythm quickened, turning raw and primal. He was like an animal claiming its mate, and I was more than willing to be claimed. I could feel the pressure building up in my lower abdomen, a bubble of pure ecstasy ready to explode any second.

"Marc... I'm—" I gasped out. He cut me off with a heated kiss, swallowing my gasp of surprise.

His hand slid down between our bodies, fingers finding my clit and rubbing in the same maddening rhythm as his strokes. "I know," he growled against my lips, eyes dark with desire. "Me too."

With every stroke of his fingers and every thrust of his hips, the bubble inside of me grew. His name was a chant on my lips, called out in desperate gasps and moans.

My body tensed under him, and he continued to drive into me with deep thrusts. Everything around me exploded into bright lights and white-hot pleasure. My mind blanked as ecstasy washed over me, shaking me to the core.

I felt Marcus' body stiffen above mine, heard his low groan as he found his own release. We collapsed together, breaths mingling in the warmed air of our tent.

My heart pounded heavily in my chest, a wild counterpoint to the gentle thump of his heartbeat beneath my cheek. I floated in the blissful aftermath of our lovemaking.

Hours later, as rain pelted against the tent, we lay together, bodies feeding off each other's warmth. Idly, I caressed my belly with trailing fingers, not yet ready to slide into sleep. It wasn't the usual curse of insomnia; I hadn't suffered from sleep deprivation since Marcus had come back into my life and spent most nights with me.

Instead, I indulged in a waking dream, one so clear I knew it was my future, reaching out to let me know everything would be okay.

In the dream, three little girls ran through the grass on the lawn where our tent now stood, chasing butterflies. Laughing and skipping, perfectly happy, alive and loved. And on the edges of my vision stood me and Marcus, arms entwined, looking on. Both of us smiling.

The End

Books of characters mentioned in this story (in reading order):

Hazel & Isaac (Secret Wife)

When Hazel Davis and Isaac Wesson reunite two years after a secret Vegas wedding meant to be annulled, they're forced to confront the Wesson-Davis family feud that tore their parents apart—as well as their undeniable chemistry...

Marlowe & Tucker (Jaded Wife)

When infertility treatments fail to help Marlowe conceive the child she desperately wants, she and husband Tucker pin their hopes on adoption—but a sinister threat and a tragic mistake threaten to destroy their marriage and lives forever...

Trina & Nassir (Tempt)

Trina Davis must choose between the stable future with her fiancé, Lamont or the intense, irresistible love of her past with

Nassir, a man bound by secrets and family duties. Can passion overcome betrayal?

Joy & Nolan (Runaway Wife)

When Nolan Christakis discovers his deceased wife Joy is actually alive and living under an assumed name, it ignites a relentless pursuit to uncover the truth behind her staged death and forces them to confront the misunderstandings that tore their marriage apart...

Kneshel & Lamont (His Gift)

When Lamont and Kneshel's paths cross again in his hometown of Valleyfield, their intense chemistry reignites, but past hurts and closely-guarded secrets threaten a future together...

Rilya & Conrad (His Muse)

He never wanted children. She never told him he had one. When Conrad Howitt discovers his best friend's sister gave birth to his daughter, he'll do anything to claim them both—even if it means marriage.

Evie & Ben (His Spark)

Evie finds herself irresistibly drawn to Ben, the infuriatingly charming firefighter who's always pushed her buttons. As their chemistry ignites, Evie must decide between safety and passion.

Epilogue 2

As I stood amid the laughter and chaos of the family celebration in Tulum, Mexico, a wave of contentment washed over me. The joyous noise of my loved ones was music to my ears, a reflection of the enduring strength of family bonds.

The golden light of the Mexican sun bathed the elegant Tulum mansion, casting a warm glow on the laughter-riddled chaos. The backyard garden buzzed with the excitement of Dad's post-nuptial celebration.

My father, Marcus Sr., had married his girlfriend Robyn in an intimate ceremony in this very backyard earlier. The sprawling mansion belonged to my sister Trina. It was one of many parting gifts Nassir had bestowed upon her years ago during a painful separation.

"Señor?" A server politely held out a glass of champagne on a silver platter, and I gratefully took it, promising to make it my last.

We'd already toasted the happy bride and groom, and the couple had performed their customary first dance. Now, the small party was winding down.

Dad and my stepmother were seated at opposite ends of the banquet table, both looking splendid in their wedding finery. Robyn's three kids were seated next to her and chatting animatedly. Nassir sat next to Dad and seemed to be making a point, using his free hand to wave around as he underscored whatever he was saying while he held his four-year-old son, Javed, securely on his lap.

If I had to guess, I'd bet the two men were arguing about cricket. Since Nassir introduced Dad to the game, they now spent half the time arguing over who they favored for the next World Cup. Nassir always insisted the South Asian teams had the best batsmen, while Dad swore the South African team had a vastly superior track record. As for me, I thought the sport went on for much too long.

The older kids, Arslan, Aisha, and Lucas, huddled around a portable TV and Wii they'd wheeled outdoors. Their fingers moved over the controllers as they raced each other on Mario Kart.

Aisha screamed, angling her body as if she was physically avoiding the obstacle on the course they were playing, while Lucas was threatening to lap Arslan again, much to his cousin's chagrin.

I grinned. I'd been a bit of a gamer myself at their age and understood deep those passions ran.

A melodic laugh carrying across the garden on the summer breeze made me turn. I spotted Lexi across the way, chatting with Hazel's husband Isaac while carrying our one-year-old daughter, Nova.

I paused for a moment, struck by the beauty of my wife holding one of the children we'd created. The sight never failed to make my heart swell.

We had built a home, nurtured careers, were raising three human babies and two fur ones. It hadn't always been easy, especially after Nova's birth, but we'd grown together.

I smiled, warmth expanding in my heart. What we'd cultivated in these years, the intimacy of truly knowing someone was what I cherished most.

My attention shifted to my eldest daughter, two-year-old Mila. She chased an endless stream of bubbles pouring from the bubble machine on the lawn with Trina's daughter, Holland, and Hazel's son, Mason.

The trio were affectionately called the Triplets since they'd all been born within the same year. The girls' rose-pink flower-girl dresses, along with Mason's smart little suit, were smeared with grass stains and mud.

There'd be no reusing those outfits.

I marveled at the simplicity of the children's joy, and how it reflected the purest form of happiness. It was a reminder of life's most ordinary moments holding the most profound meaning.

"Daddy, look me," said Mila. She was now holding up a cluster of soap bubbles.

As I made my way to her, the bubbles popped in her tiny hands. Her expression was one of surprised dismay, and I hastened to her to comfort her.

"It's okay, Milabean. You can catch some more." I was relieved when all she did was laugh and return to the chase.

"Your daughter is an angel," Trina said as she approached, cradling my six-week-old daughter Jade in her arms. "I've never met a quieter baby." She swayed as she held her. "You sure you didn't do the Benadryl thing to keep her quiet?"

I knew she was kidding, but I gave her a glare anyway. "I'm going to pretend you didn't say that."

She shoved me with her shoulder and grinned. "All I'm saying is, I wish mine had been this quiet at this age. With Holland, you could hear her bawl from one end of the yacht to another at that age."

"When did we become such grown-ups?" I mused, watching the kids with a wistful smile.

"Speak for yourself," Trina teased, her eyes dancing with youthful mischief. "I'm still twenty-one at heart."

I grinned at her cheeky remark. "And yet, you're the one who dreamed of becoming a mom at...ten, remember?"

Trina's soft laugh was drowned out by the rhythmic beat of the reggaeton over the speakers. She nodded, her gaze drifting over to her daughter Holland, and there was pride in her eyes.

I let my gaze wander back over to Lexi. She was dancing now, holding Nova in her arms and swaying to the rhythm of the music.

Nova's little hands were wrapped around Lexi's neck, her tiny head bobbing along with the music. I couldn't help but feel a twinge of amusement and affection as I watched them. My daughters would be better dancers than me.

Lexi's smile, even though Nova's head obscured much of her face was a sight I would never tire of seeing. Her love for our kids, for our life together, was visible in her every movement.

"Almost makes me want to try for another girl," Trina said, bringing my attention back to her. She was now looking down at Jade with a soft smile.

"Go for it, sis. I'm done making Davises." I reflected on the decision Lexi and I had made to close the *baby juice* factory by undergoing a vasectomy three weeks ago.

"I hope so," Trina said, "because Lexi's body deserves a break. That girl has been pregnant four years in a row." As she said this, I noticed my sister's side-eye, as though it was all my fault.

"Got that right," Hazel said, arriving with her hands out to get her own cuddles from Jade. Trina handed the baby over to Hazel.

I felt a ripple of irritation, but before I could voice it, I was cut off by another voice. "I didn't judge Hazel for having a five-year age gap between Lucas and Mason. And Trina, I didn't judge you for having a geriatric pregnancy with Holland." Lexi shook her head, braids swaying, and repositioned Nova higher on her hip. "So why judge me?"

Everyone looked at her in surprise, not expecting such a fiery defense. I exchanged stunned looks with my sisters.

Eager to smooth things over, I relieved Lexi of Nova, holding the baby against my chest. With my other arm, I pulled Lexi into my embrace, delighting in the sugary scent of her shampoo.

"You okay, my love?" I asked before pressing a kiss onto the tip of her nose.

Lexi chewed on her lip, seemingly too miffed to answer. Trina took a step closer to Lexi. "You're right," she said humbly. "I was out of line. I'm sorry for offending you."

Next to me, Hazel nodded in agreement. "I'm sorry, too."

Lexi's features softened, and she looked equally contrite. She plucked a glass of cold sparkling water with a lemon twist from one of the passing servers.

"I didn't mean to snap," she told them. "Postpartum hormones, maybe." Her lips curved apologetically. "Am fed up with everyone commenting on how quickly our daughters came to us. I was very much aware of what would happen when I had unprotected sex with your brother."

Trina burst out laughing, and Hazel joined her. I chuckled. The tension was broken. Lexi's lips twitched upwards into a small smile, and she took a sip of her water.

"Fair point," Trina conceded. "And for the record, you both make beautiful babies."

I took in how gorgeous my wife looked on this special day, with her braids intertwined with river pearls and her satin designer dress embracing her gorgeous curves. After three children, her body was even more lush, and I couldn't look at her without thinking of what it felt like to hold her against me, stroke her, sink into her.

"And we wouldn't change a thing about our lives," I added, pulling Lexi closer. A feeling of deep contentment washed over me at her familiar, comforting touch.

I exhaled, tightening my hold on her. This right here—my family surrounding me, Lexi's steadfast presence was my happiness.

Lexi took a sip from her glass, her gaze sliding toward me. Our eyes met, and I could see the world I loved in her beautiful brown depths, a world of warmth and love and family.

I didn't even have the words to express how much more I loved her now than I had before, and how proud I was of my strong, loving, spirited wife. Pride and love made my chest swell, and I leaned forward and kissed her again, this time on her full, beautiful mouth.

The air puffed past her lips as she sighed against my mouth. My heart swelled with the knowledge that she was mine, body and soul, just as I was hers.

I hated seeing her subjected to such scrutiny and judgment. The speed of our reproduction was nobody's business but ours, and I bristled whenever family members and friends voiced those comments in regards to my beautiful, brave wife.

"I adore my nieces, and I'll love any more that come along," Trina put in.

Lexi touched Nova's cheek. The toddler, who had drowsed against my shoulder, wrinkled her nose but didn't open her eyes.

"We didn't mean to make you feel attacked," Hazel said, stroking Jade's chubby cheek. The baby wriggled in Hazel's arms, her dark eyes wide as she gazed up at her aunt. A gummy smile spread across her face as she made a small cooing noise.

Lexi laughed softly at Jade's reaction. "She loves Titi Hazel."

Trina turned to Lexi, her expression serious. "I'm really sorry, Lex."

"We worry about you," Hazel explained, cradling Jade close to her chest and swaying on the spot.

Lexi reached out, placing her hand on Hazel's arm. "I know you both do," she said. "And I love you for it. But believe me, Marcus and I got this."

Hazel added, "We love you, Lexi. You brought my brother back to me."

I detected the glimmer of moisture in Lexi's eyes right before the three women hugged each other tightly.

"We want in on the hugging," Isaac announced as he approached with Nassir. He slipped an arm affectionately around Hazel's waist. She grinned up at him.

There was a shriek as Holland clasped a large bubble with both hands, only to have it pop and squirt soap into her eye. Nassir loped across the garden and returned with his daughter in his arms.

"It's time to turn off the bubble machine," Nassir said firmly. "The grass is slick with soap. They've had enough."

"Let's take the kids down to the beach so the moms can have some quiet," added Isaac.

Nassir and I murmured in agreement.

"Sounds like a plan," I said. "For after I dance with my lovely wife."

I transferred my slumbering daughter Nova into Isaac's waiting arms, then I turned to Lexi. "May I have this dance, Mrs. Davis?" I held out my hand, palm up.

She laughed, a sweet, soft sound that had my heart waltzing before we hit the dance floor. "Always," she said, placing her hand in mine.

As we moved, I whispered into her ear, "Have I told you today how stunning you look?" I pressed a tender kiss to her temple.

"Only about fifty times," she said.

I stroked her waist. "Well, it's still true. I like how you handled my sisters. You never cease to impress me."

Lexi's voice was soft. "I meant everything I said."

"This past year hasn't been easy, but you've handled it all with grace and strength that leaves me in awe." I pulled back to see her reaction. Her eyes shimmered with unshed tears, but she was smiling, so radiant it made my heart ache.

Lexi squeezed my hand in response, leaning in to press her forehead against my chest. "You make all of it worth it," she whispered back.

I drew her in closer and fused our lips, heedless of our surroundings. In this moment, it was just the two of us, anchored together.

Author's Note

I was writing Trina and Nassir's final story (Trust) when Lexi and MJ showed up, and their magnetic connection and steaming passion completely derailed everything! MJ's tale was never on my agenda since neither he nor Lexi spoke much or (I probably shouldn't say this) seemed interesting during their appearances in other books.

But these two found their way into my heart and writing their love story turned out to be an absolute joy. Seeing Lexi's reserved warmth chip away at MJ's aloof façade kept me grinning through every chapter. Watching them realize how perfectly their hearts complemented each other? Swoon!

I hope you enjoyed experiencing the delightful twists and turns of their journey to HEA as much as I delighted in writing it. This couple surprised me, charmed me, and will always have a special place in my heart.

If you want to chat more about books, share your favorite moments from His Heart, or just follow along for all the behind-the-scenes fun, you can find me on all the socials!

Thank you, as always, for reading!

Xoxo,

Niomie R.